T0354683

Not Dead but Almost

Not Dead but Almost

A NOVEL IN THREE PARTS

TIMOTHY BENSON

NOT DEAD BUT ALMOST
A NOVEL IN THREE PARTS

iUniverse books may be ordered through booksellers or by contacting:

iUniverse
1663 Liberty Drive
Bloomington, IN 47403
www.iuniverse.com
844-349-9409

Because of the dynamic nature of the Internet, any web addresses or links contained in this book may have changed since publication and may no longer be valid. The views expressed in this work are solely those of the author and do not necessarily reflect the views of the publisher, and the publisher hereby disclaims any responsibility for them.

Any people depicted in stock imagery provided by Getty Images are models, and such images are being used for illustrative purposes only. Certain stock imagery © Getty Images.

ISBN: 978-1-6632-6993-5 (sc)
ISBN: 978-1-6632-6994-2 (e)

Library of Congress Control Number: 2024927172

Print information available on the last page.

iUniverse rev. date: 12/27/2024

City of Dust

Welcome to Encino

"Nobody comes here on purpose, not anymore." The sadness in the man's voice was obvious.

It was his response to my comment about how the town looked strangely quiet, almost abandoned. The road into town was lined with one old, unoccupied building after another. There was a small, boarded-up motel right next to the run down gas station where the man was filling my tank. I went back to looking down the hill at the main street of Encino. Just two blocks long, Railroad Street was lined on both sides with a mix of old, weathered adobe and clapboard-sided buildings. A lot of them were two and three stories but some were small, one-story buildings sitting shoulder to shoulder along empty, broken sidewalks. Traffic lights at the two intersections were hanging over the broken asphalt, unlit and unnecessary. Central New Mexico is dotted with quaint, small towns, towns full of life and color. Encino looked like it was once one of them, but not anymore.

I turned back toward the man. His sun-weathered face and sweat-stained denim shirt were reminders to me of how much time I spent indoors at a desk. "When I was a kid my father used to drive here on business, He came here for years and years. He sold mining equipment and lubricants. I remember him saying how much he enjoyed his time here and telling me what a nice, little town Encino was."

"Used to be." the man replied. He was tall and reed thin and the slouch in his posture mirrored the sad tone of his voice. He looked like a man who'd been defeated. "I grew up here and it's not the same place." A name patch on his shirt read "Jack". That was all I knew about him and somehow I felt sorry for the guy.

When I'd left Albuquerque that morning my plan had been to take Interstate 40 straight to Santa Rosa for my meeting with a photographer. A side trip to Encino had been a totally impulsive decision, a way to tap into the memories my late father had shared with me over the years. His recent death was still gnawing at me. As I stood there gazing down the hill at what was left of a once-charming little town it was hard to connect his stories with what I was looking at.

I heard the click of the gas pump when it reached the full mark and then the man's voice. "So, anythin' else for you today?"

I hesitated before answering, "Uh, no, Jack, I guess not but can you suggest a place I can get a cup of coffee?"

He took a moment to look over my Lexus SUV and seemed to draw a conclusion. "Well, I hope you don't mean Starbucks cause there's just Rita's Café down the street." He turned and pointed down the hill. "See those two pick-ups parked down there? They're right in front of the café. Don't worry about the parkin' meters, they don't work anymore."

We walked under the faded, old Texaco sign and into the customer area to finish our transaction. While Jack ran my credit card I looked around the messy room and something caught my eye. It was a clean, perfectly pressed police uniform on a hanger, including a tan Stetson and a pair of shiny black boots on the floor below it. I leaned in and saw that the badge read "Encino Police Department" and below it "Chief". Jack saw me studying it and said, "That's mine. That was my old job, back when the town still had enough money to pay me."

"So who's the police chief now?"

"Well, I guess it's still me because I never officially resigned. I keep the uniform in case I need it someday. You never know. You just never know. Now I just run this place and my Dad's old repair shop next door."

I looked out the window at the small clapboard building and the large three-bay garage behind it.

"My father used to fix equipment for the mine and just about anythin' else that needed repair around here." He looked out the window and said, "Now the whole god-damned town is broken." He pointed out the window on the other side. "I used to keep an eye on that old motel there but the owner gave up on the place so I did too." The sad tone to his voice had an angry edge to it. He handed me my credit card and receipt. "Thanks, uh,

Mr. Rorbach." I nodded, took another look at the uniform and walked back to my car.

I drove slowly down the hill, glancing to the right then the left at the ghosts of businesses that used to form downtown Encino. I thought how similar it looked to Old Town Albuquerque with its Spanish charm. But the buildings had lost some of that appeal. Their chipped, faded signs had once beckoned people to come inside for groceries, hardware, clothing and all the things of life. I could almost hear them talking and laughing. Even the large Catholic church on the corner seemed just a shadow of its former beauty. A few of the storefronts were covered with plywood but for the most part it looked as though the people in the town had just closed their doors behind them and left. In my mind I tried to match what I was looking at to some of the old photographs my father had taken on his visits. The once colorful streetscape looked old and worn out. I began to understand the sadness in Jack's voice.

Except for a rusty Volkswagen one block farther down, the two pickups were the only vehicles on the street. I pulled over and parked behind them. There was a certain Mexican flavor to the facade of Rita's Café. The white stucco wall featured a graceful brick arch over the carved oak entrance door. Large black iron and glass light fixtures flanked the entry niche. Like everything else I'd seen since my arrival, a thin layer of dust coated it all. A bell jingled as I opened the door and when I stepped inside I knew I was looking at exactly the same little café that my father had probably visited. The scuffed up black and white tile floor was bordered in back by a long laminate counter and a row of red vinyl and chrome stools. Matching tables and chairs sat empty along the front window and two large, round tables filled the middle of the floor. The menu board behind the counter looked original. An array of old black and white photos of the mine and local folks hung on every available section of wall. It was like I had stepped back in time.

Two tanned and grizzled old men sat at a corner table, nursing their coffees and giving me a thorough looking over as I walked to the counter and chose a stool. I sat there for longer than my normal supply of patience allowed and they never took their eyes off me. Finally a stocky, middle-aged Hispanic woman stepped through the kitchen door. "Good morning," she said in a voice as sad as Jack's. Her eyes were just as sad too but somehow she managed a slight smile. I had the feeling that smiles didn't come easy for her. Still, it was enough to put me at ease. "Good morning," I answered, "how's your coffee?"

"Just made a fresh pot. I like it strong so I hope that's okay with you."

"That's the way I make it too".

She stepped away to the back counter and then returned with the pot and a cup. Before I could ask her for a to-go cup she started pouring and set a menu in front of me. "I can make you some breakfast if you order it right away. It's almost lunchtime." She sighed and said, "I never know when I'm gonna get a few customers" She noticed how the two men were still staring at me and said, "I guess I should apologize for those boys. We don't see a lot of new faces around here anymore and it looks like you're today's entertainment."

I glanced at them over my shoulder. "Oh, that's okay" I was getting more and more curious about this tired ghost of a town. It was looking like I'd be spending a little more time in Encino than I'd planned on.

"I'll be back there in the kitchen for a while," she said with a sigh. "Just shout if you need anything. I'm Rita by the way."

Sipping coffee and gazing out at the empty street made me lose track of the time. It was going on noon and it was clear that I wouldn't make it to Santa Rosa in time for my meeting. I pulled my phone from my pocket and called the photographer. His phone rang three times and I was getting ready to leave a voicemail when he answered, "Hey, Jay, what's up?"

"Morning, Saul. Hey, I'm running late and wanted to see if we could push our meeting back a little."

"Sure, my afternoon is pretty loose, just the way I like it. Where are you now?"

"I'm in Encino."

There was silence at the other end, then, "What in the hell are you doing there?"

I felt strangely embarrassed. "Well, it was just a spur of the moment thing. I saw the sign on the highway and remembered all the stuff my Dad used to tell me about his trips here so I thought I'd check it out. It sure isn't much of a town anymore."

"You got that right. It's called City of Dust. I thought that place was dead."

I suddenly wondered if the two men in the corner could hear my voice so I changed the subject. "Any idea of the drive time to your place?"

"Oh, it's at least fifty miles, maybe longer. Take 60 up to the 54 and then it's a straight shot to here. I'd figure an hour plus. There's just a whole lot of nothing in between." He paused then added, "Just like in Encino."

"Okay, let's say one o'clock or close to it."

"Sounds good. I have the stills ready for you to look at now. I had to deal with a couple of nervous Navajo when I was taping on the reservation last week but the video will be edited by the time you get here. You can take everything back with you to add your voice-over."

"My deadline for the script isn't until Thursday afternoon so I know I can get the finished work done for my Friday meeting in LA. I've got the rough copy done and my voice-overs are scripted so I think we're in good shape. See you later."

I called out to Rita for a check. We chatted awhile, mostly small talk about the mine, the town and the loss of so many of her friends and neighbors. Her tone was almost a lament and she seemed to share Jack's feelings about the town's demise. She added a few snide comments about the mining operation and the people who ran it. Her sad tone was tinged with anger.

A few minutes later I was back in my car. The road to get back on to Route 60 was behind me but first I turned around and took a slow drive down Railroad Street to see the rest of the downtown. I put the window down and set my phone camera on video. There was another small church and I saw an empty school on one of the side streets. Beyond it were rows of empty looking houses on both sides. There wasn't a person in sight. I turned around at the last cross street and was driving back up the hill when I noticed an old hotel nestled between two empty storefronts. There were lights on inside and the sign looked to be in fairly good condition. It looked like the Bond Hotel was still open for business. I parked that thought in the back of my mind and headed to Santa Rosa.

Sometimes Pictures Lie

For a guy who'd spent years setting and meeting deadlines, having a laser focus on my work had always served me well. That focus wasn't as strong when I walked into my home office the next day. I'd been drifting back and forth between working on the Indian documentary and thoughts of Encino and of course my father. On his last trip there just a little over two years ago he'd experienced a whole different town than I had. My documentary was on stolen Native American artifacts so everything that filled my mind that day had to do with unanswered questions from the past. How did those native treasures disappear? How did a once thriving small town come to its deathbed?

That evening after Katie and I finished dinner I asked her, "Do you remember where we put that box of Dad's old memorabilia?"

"I think it's in that tall cabinet in the garage." She paused and seemed to be studying my face. "Jay, it's only been a few weeks, are you sure you're ready?"

"Yeah, I think so. There are a few things I'm really curious about."

I brought the box inside and set it on the dining room table. Katie brought in two glasses of wine and we sat down on opposite sides of the table. She knew it might turn out to be an emotional activity for me and I was glad she wanted to share it. "Are you looking for something in particular?" she asked.

I wasn't sure how to answer her. I thought for a moment then said, "Not really. I hadn't thought much about this stuff until I made that little side trip to Encino. Now I can't stop thinking about it."

"What's that have to do with your Dad's box of stuff?"

"I'm not sure, maybe nothing at all." I took a sip of wine and opened the box. "After Mom died Dad never went anywhere without his camera. He was sad and he said he wanted to record every memory and every person he met along the way. So I'm looking for any photographs he might have taken when he was on the road."

We sorted through the box, making small piles on the table. My father was a very organized man and the contents were in separate manila envelopes, each one clearly labeled and dated. That made my task much easier. We were about two thirds of the way through the box when I pulled out a thick envelope marked VAUGHN ENCINO CLOVIS 2022. Katie must have seen something on my face and asked, "Is that what you're looking for?"

I stared at the envelope. "Yeah, I think this is it."

I cleared some space on the table and spread out the contents; small bundles of snapshots each with a paper label and neatly wrapped with a rubber band. "Geez, Dad, you sure loved the details," I muttered. Three of the labels read ENCINO. I pushed the other stacks aside and unwrapped the first of the three. I flipped through the photos in silence as Katie came around and sat beside me. Since the camera belonged to my Dad he was the photographer and appeared only in a few of the photos. There were a few shots of the mountains and the copper mine but most of them were pictures of various places and people around Encino. It was clear that his many visits over the years had brought him friends and good times.

"See anything familiar?" Katie asked.

"Yeah, I recognize a lot of the buildings. They sure have aged in just a few years. Like this shot, that's the main drag, Railroad Street. Almost all of those buildings are empty now. And check out all those people on the streets. There wasn't a soul walking around when I was there."

"What do you think happened?"

"I have no idea but I did some searching online and found out Encino had over two thousand people back then. Now, as of last week, there are only forty-two, at least that's what a waitress told me."

"How could something like that happen so fast? It's kind of spooky."

"I agree." Dad's photos hadn't revealed much until I got near the end of the first stack. Someone else had used the camera to take a photo of my Dad with two other men. I thought again of how much I resembled him. Both of us were tall and lean with brown eyes. Even our crooked smiles were the same. In the photo the men were standing in front of a long, ornate bar hoisting their glasses. A reflection in the mirror behind them showed part of a sign. The image was in reverse but I could still read it, "Bond Hotel". I showed it to Katie.

A slight smile appeared. "The town, all of it, looked so normal back then and your Dad was right smack in the middle of things."

I laid two of the street photos in front of her and then handed her my phone. This is a video from yesterday. It's the downtown, the same street as in the photos." I watched her face as she looked back and forth from the video to the photos.

"That almost gives me goosebumps," she said, handing me back my phone. "All of that happened in a little over two years but it looks like it was twenty." She shook her head. "What happened to those two thousand people?"

I just shrugged. I couldn't take my eyes off the photos. There was my Dad laughing with friends in a town full of life and activity. It was as though my visit had been somewhere else. I didn't know what it all meant but something inside me pushed toward an idea I'd had right before I'd left Encino. The Bond Hotel might be a place to find some answers.

I was able to meet my Thursday deadline for the Indian documentary and I was proud of the finished production. It was my first attempt at the big leagues of television. I took a cheap, red-eye flight to LA on Friday morning and that afternoon, on a flat-screen TV in a ridiculously large conference room, I screened *A Stolen Heritage* for two people from *The History Channel* and four representatives from the Hopi and Navajo nations. Their smiles and nodding heads told me that Saul and I had done a good job. But even with all that, Encino kept finding its way back into my thoughts. By the time the screening was over I'd mentally come up with a very loose framework for my next project; *Encino: Not Dead but Almost*.

After the screening I went back to my hotel and put together a rough outline of a documentary. That evening, over drinks and dinner, I laid out my idea to a curator and producer from the network. It was long on mystery and short on specifics but they were as intrigued by the dying little town as I was. We talked about costs and the calendar and by the time we'd wrapped up the social part of the evening I had a handshake deal to proceed along with a promise of a little seed money.

It was another reminder of how glad I was that Katie had such a great career. Her work in administration at UNM Health and the salary that went with it was a great cushion against my own sometimes uncertain cash flow. My degree in History with a minor in Journalism gave me a great foundation for creating documentaries but a freelance writer in a gig economy doesn't always have a stable income. Payment for *A Stolen Heritage* was my first big professional score and my Encino project would bring me a livable wage over the next few months. There were incentives in my deal for extra fees based upon content and potential viewer ratings that *History Channel* marketing people would determine. But at the moment I had no idea what my story would be; a small, American town left behind by progress or something more. Only time would tell.

It took an entire day of trading voicemails with Saul before we finally connected. Not surprisingly a fellow gig-worker like him was as ready for a new project as I was. I tried a light approach when I started my sales pitch. "So, how would you like to meet me for a fun day in Encino?"

He laughed, hesitated and said, "You and Encino again. What is it with you and that dreary place?"

"It's hard to explain. When a town practically disappears in just a couple of years it doesn't seem normal. The people at *History Channel* agreed and gave me the go-ahead to check it out."

"Just a go-ahead, no money?"

"Relax. They're giving me a small advance to get started and I can pay you for a day or two's worth of work until we get rolling."

"If we get rolling. What's your plan?

It was a question I didn't yet have an answer for. All I could say was, "Meet me there day after tomorrow and I'll walk you through it. Ten o'clock at the old Texaco station as you get into town." He agreed. I had just forty-eight hours to figure out what the hell I was going to do.

Just Looking Around

Fortunately the Albuquerque outbound morning traffic was light and I made it to Encino in ninety minutes. Living in a place like New Mexico, where I was constantly surrounded by landscapes and impossibly blue skies that looked like Georgia O'Keefe paintings made it hard to feel a need to hurry on the highway. The natural beauty was everywhere. When I reached the Texaco station Saul was already there waiting in his Jeep on the side of the lot next to the old motel. He'd left the top down for his drive from Santa Rosa and the wind had done a number on his long hair. I could see Jack standing in the window, watching us. When I pulled up to the pump he came out the door and headed my way. Saul got out of his Jeep and joined us.

I didn't wait to see if Jack remembered me. "Hi. Jack, I'm back." He nodded, remembered my Lexus and said, "Gas and coffee I suppose."

While he pumped I said to Saul, "Glad you could make it."

"I wouldn't have missed it for the world." His sarcasm was clear. I winced and nodded toward Jack as a signal to Saul that he should avoid bad-mouthing the town. He nodded in return.

Jack looked at me. "So you guys have business here this mornin', do ya'?"

Saul looked at me with a "say something" kind of look.

"Well, sort of." I answered. "When I was here last week I got kind of curious about this place, Encino, and I told my friend here. We just want to look around and maybe take a few photographs."

Jack looked at me and then Saul. "Well, there's not much left to see."

"How about the mine, it's still operating isn't it?"

"Hard to say exactly. It's sort of runnin' but almost nobody works there anymore. Just a handful of guys and they pretty much keep to themselves. They stay in the houses that American owns on the north edge of town, They come into town to drink, mostly, and for coffee and gas once in awhile."

Saul finally joined the conversation. "If I want to use my video camera is there any action in the pit, like digging and that kind of thing?"

Jack shook his head. "Nope, I haven't seen a sky full of dust in a long time, not like we used to. We saw it every day. But I'll tell ya' one thing, we sure don't miss all the damn blastin'."

"Is the mine still in business?" I asked.

Jack hesitated. He looked kind of nervous. "Nobody will talk about that. The mine people, that's American Minin' and Extraction, they're based in Denver. The office guys used to be here all the time. It was good for business. But they don't come around much anymore, hardly ever. The guy who's in charge here in Encino is Boyce Hammond. He's got a really small crew with him, like I said just a handful of guys. Everyone else got let go about two years ago."

Saul and I looked at each other, both of us confused and curious. "How do you run a huge copper mine with just a handful of guys?" I asked Jack.

"That's been the big question around here ever since they announced the layoffs. They didn't say much, just that the amount of copper left in the ground didn't justify keepin' the pit goin'. They're supposedly doin' somethin' called decommissionin'. It's a law that says they have to put the land back to normal." He stopped and pulled the nozzle from my tank. "It really pisses me off. The company doesn't tell us nothin' and Hammond and his boys keep to themselves except for their trips into town. They gotta get their gas here from me but I can't get em' to say much."

We walked into the station to pay and Saul asked, "So besides a few miners who else lives here?"

"Just us lifers. We grew up here and got no place else to go. Even a few of the ranchers sold out and moved on. There's a couple of small farmer's hangin' on but who knows how long they can last? It's hard to say how much longer this town will be here." The sadness had returned to his voice and so had the anger. "Man. it's like dominos. The miners and their families left which meant we didn't have kids to fill the school so the teachers left. The store owners couldn't make a livin' so they closed along with most of the other businesses. The churches were empty on Sunday so they closed their doors. Some of the people who hung on for awhile got tired of drivin' to Vaughn or Clovis to buy necessities so they moved on. Hell, those of us who are left have to haul our own garbage to the landfill." He turned and pointed out the window. "Just look down the street. That's all that's left."

I don't think I'd ever seen a man look and sound so painfully sad. I had to change the subject. "Well, thanks for the info, Jack. We appreciate it." He finished with the transaction and handed me back my credit card. I saw Saul staring at the police uniform. "Come on, man." I said and tugged on his sleeve. "Thanks again, Jack."

As we walked out the door Jack called out, "Hey, if you're drivin' up to the mine watch that road. It can be pretty rough."

"Sounds like we better take my Jeep." Saul said. "You drive so I can handle the camera." I tossed my laptop bag on to the floor behind the seat and we climbed in.

My first thought was to stop at the café and say hello to Rita but I decided to do it later. I tried to maintain a slow and steady speed as we drove down Railroad Street and then turned on to a few of the side streets. Saul had his video camera wedged tightly against his shoulder, saying nothing. Even though I'd already driven through the downtown this trip was no less sad and strangely fascinating. The working title of my project kept intruding on my thoughts; *Not Dead but Almost.*

When we passed under the second dark traffic light Saul lowered the camera. "We'll go up the other side of the street on our way back. I want to see where the people lived. Let's head for the mine."

Throughout history cities and towns were located for good reasons. The surrounding land was fertile. A nearby river could be used for transport. A growing railroad network needed a hub. But mines were located for one reason and one reason only; that's where the ore was. It didn't matter how hot and dry the climate or how rough the terrain, there was the ore so there was the mine. Encino had started out as a sleepy, little farming and ranching town and that was all. When the mine opened it was reborn to serve the people that came with the operation. Like so many other towns it became dependent on its biggest employer.

The photography side of the project was Saul's and when we reached the edge of the downtown area he told me to pull over. I pulled into the driveway of an empty looking house. He got out, lifted a canvas tarp and said, "I want to use my new toy." I joined him and stood by while he took out a shiny, white drone and set it on the concrete. "This has the kind of range we'll need. We need a view of this God-forsaken place that's not from street level." A few minutes later we watched the drone slowly rise to a level above the roof tops and hover. "I'm going to take it up to three hundred feet so we can get a really wide perspective on the size of the place."

For half an hour Saul steered that airborne camera around, getting into parts of the town we'd never be able to get to on foot. The higher altitude shots gave us a good idea of how remote the little town felt in the middle of ranch country. The drone made lower level passes and we got views of the empty houses with empty yards and dead gardens. We could almost feel the loneliness the former towns people must have felt. When he was satisfied he'd gotten enough coverage he brought his expensive toy back in for a landing. A few minutes later we headed for the mine.

A stop sign riddled with bullet holes greeted us at the end of the street. Railroad Street intersected with what had once been a smooth, paved two-lane road. It was now rutted and littered with gravel and broken asphalt. The street sign had faded so badly it was unreadable so Saul decided on the name Shit Street. A large metal sign on the side of the hill read "American Mining – Encino Works" with an arrow pointing to the right. I turned the steering wheel and warned, "Get a quick shot of that sign and then hang on, man, this looks like it's gonna be a thrill ride."

A few hundred yards later we passed a large water tower with the spray painted message "I'm Outta Here". Another slow, bumpy mile farther into the drive the broken pavement of Shit Street turned into a badly graded dirt road and I was glad we were in the Jeep instead of my car. The road rose gradually, winding through a combination of outcroppings, native brush and piles of dirt and rocks from when the road was first built. About ten minutes later we reached the crest of a large hill and stopped. Stretched out in front of us was the vast expanse of the open-pit mine. It was easy to read its history from the individual terraced shelves of reddish-brown dirt, each one a separate two years of activity.

In an active mine the shelves would serve as a spiraling road for the graders and trucks. They moved the raw ore up from the bottom tray to the leach pads and processing tanks that start the extraction process. My father's photos had shown four leach pads and three tanks but since then one of the tanks had been moved closer to a shaft in the side of the hill. But even with that there was no sign of trucks or working equipment of any kind, A few trucks were neatly parked at the very bottom of the pit and the small office shack was still sitting beside the shaft. We got out of the Jeep and I walked to the edge of the cut while Saul spent a few minutes panning his camera over the view below. "Nothing left but a big hole in the ground." I said.

Saul walked back to the Jeep and exchanged his video camera for a tripod and still camera. "Here, set this up over on that flat area. There's a pair of binoculars in that green case if you want a better look." While I followed his request he got his drone airborne again and maneuvered it in a wide loop around the entire perimeter of the pit. It only took about fifteen minutes and after he'd stashed it back in the Jeep he joined me on the rim.

For the next half hour we viewed, photographed and discussed the mine. We didn't pretend to be geologists or mining experts but one thing we both agreed on was that the mine didn't appear to be as deep as other open-pit operations we'd seen in photographs. It looked like things had stopped somewhere in the middle. The untouched area of the mine looked identical in color to the portion already dug out. It seemed that if the copper veins had run out, like American Mining had told the people of Encino, there would be some kind of visible difference. A thought came to me. "Hang on a second. I have some of my Dad's old photos in my bag. I want to check something."

I dug through the contents of the bag and pulled out the envelope of pictures. A minute later I found the one I was looking for, a shot of the mine taken from a vantage point very close to where we were standing. I walked back to the rim, held the photo out in front of me and compared it to the view below. They were almost identical. Saul walked over, stood beside me and said exactly what I was thinking. "Looks like nothing has changed."

"That's what I thought too. My Dad took this picture a little over two years ago, before they announced the closing. Look closely and you can see all those trucks and graders working all over the bottom ledge." I stopped and looked down at the mine, counting the ledges then did the same thing with the photo. "They must have shut down within days or weeks from when my Dad was here last."

Saul studied the photo, looked at the mine then back at the photo. "Hey, check it out. See those pickups parked in the back corner near that tunnel in the side of the hill, by that shack? Look down there, the same trucks are there now. Why do you suppose people would still be hanging around this place two years after it closed? Jack said there were only a couple of guys left."

I put the binoculars to my eyes and scanned the corner at the base of a cliff. The large tunnel in the side of the dig looked to be large enough for an earthmover or truck to fit through. It looked like it was totally separate from the main dig below. The pickups definitely looked like the same ones in the photo and I saw something else. A man in an orange safety vest and yellow hardhat was looking back at us through binoculars. I turned toward Saul. "We're being watched."

Saul peered through his camera. The huge telephoto lens was as powerful as the binoculars. He took a breath, I heard the shutter click and he said, "Got him."

The man lowered his binoculars, turned and seemed to call out to someone. He returned to watching us and a moment later a second man exited the shack and joined him. It was an awkward situation so I did all I could think of, I waved to them. There was no response. The binocular standoff continued for another minute or so then the second man walked over to a white pickup. We watched as he headed down a small driveway until he went behind an outcropping and disappeared from our view.

Saul started to detach his camera from the tripod. "I have a feeling he's headed our way. Maybe we should pack it in for the day."

"We aren't trespassing. I didn't see any signs that said keep out."

"I know but if they're watching the rim with binoculars it must not be business as usual down there. Something doesn't smell right." His nervousness was clear.

We stashed our equipment in the Jeep and headed back down the rough road, me at the wheel and driving a bit faster than we had on the way up to the rim. We were approaching Shit Street when the white pickup, on a spur road, sped past us in the opposite direction. I looked into the rearview mirror and saw his brake lights. The road was too narrow for him to easily turn around on so it took him a few backup tries before he was on Shit Street and pointed in our direction. By then we were approaching the turn back on to Railroad Street.

We drove slowly through town. My eyes scanned from left to right while Saul kept his eyes on the rearview mirror. When I saw the sign for the Bond Hotel I pulled to the curb in front of it.

"Why are you stopping here?" Saul asked.

"Just a hunch. Let's go in here and see if that pickup comes by. I want to see how hard he'll try to find us."

"Okay, just pull up in front of a window so I can keep an eye on my equipment." As he stepped out on to the sidewalk he asked, "What do we do if he finds us and wants to know what we're doing?"

I had wondered the same thing. "I guess we'll find out if and when it happens."

A Stop at The Bond

The ornately carved front door was the first sign that in its heyday The Bond Hotel was something special in an otherwise ordinary town. When we stepped inside there were even more to take in. Brass and cut-glass light fixtures hung from the stamped tin ceiling. Oak wainscot wrapped around the entire lobby and the long registration desk. Through a large arched opening in the far wall I saw the lounge and the beautiful bar that my father had stood in front of in his photos.

Saul looked around the lobby. "I know I'm only the photographer on this little project but what in the hell is going on? Why are we doing all this?"

I didn't have a plan or an idea of any kind. I answered, "Hang on a second." and walked over to the front window just as the white pickup slowly drove by. The driver was looking at the hotel and I didn't know if he could see us in the window. I half expected him to stop but was relieved when he kept going and turned down a side street. I turned back to Saul. "Like I told you the other day, we're looking around to see why this town sort of dried up and all but disappeared so quickly. Things like that don't just happen overnight but, somehow, in this case that's exactly what happened."

"So we're up there taking pictures of the mine, a couple of guys see us and then one comes after us."

"We don't know that for sure. It might just be coincidence that he was heading into town anyway,"

"Then why did he take a different road and catch up with us on the hill? It seems to me that we were exactly what he was looking for. I didn't sign on for any kind of trouble."

I didn't understand it any more than Saul did. We were interrupted when a tall, lanky well dressed man walked in from the barroom. His gray hair and neatly trimmed beard gave him an air of dignity that seemed out of place in the little town. "Oh, I thought I heard voices. I'm Russell, the owner. What can I do for you gentlemen?"

I was caught off guard and all I could come up with for a reply was, "Oh, we're just passing through and we wondered where we could get some lunch."

Russell seemed satisfied. "Well, if you go up the hill a ways there's Rita's is on the other side of the street."

Part of me wanted to leave but a bigger part wanted a few answers. "Thanks, we'll give it a try. I paused then added, "We came in here because my Dad used to stay here when he came to town on business."

"Who's your Dad? I got to know the regulars here over the years."

"Tom Rorbach. He worked for States Oil, sold lubricants and materials to the mine. I'm Jay."

Russell hesitated for a moment then replied, "Oh yeah, I remember him, a real nice fella, always in a good mood when he stayed with us. He loved hanging out at that bar with anyone who wandered in." He paused for a few seconds then added, "You know you look a lot like him."

The hanging out at the bar comment sounded exactly like my Dad. "He really liked your place so I thought I'd check it out."

"How's he doing? Haven't seen him in quite a while."

"He was retired. He passed away a few weeks ago." It was still hard for me to say it out loud.

"Oh gee, I'm sorry. I really liked him."

I had to change the mood quickly. "So, Russell, let me ask you something. What happened around here? My Dad used to say Encino was a nice little town full of nice people. I've driven through a few times and it looks like everyone is gone, or almost everyone."

He held back from answering for a moment and nodded as he walked over and leaned on the registration desk. Finally he answered, "It's not easy for us locals to talk about. We used to have a town and now we don't." He paused again then said, "Truth be told it's that god damned mine."

"Because they closed?" I asked.

"Not just that they closed, it was how they did it. It was like one day everything was normal and the next day, boom, they're shutting down. Nobody saw it coming, including the miners."

I looked over at Saul, who didn't show much interest in joining the conversation. "My friend and I were up looking at the mine today and it looked like things just stopped in the middle. I'm no expert but I've seen mines in Arizona and Nevada that were a hell of a lot deeper."

Saul finally jumped in but not to chat with us. "That white pick-up is back!" He was looking out the window and Russell and I walked over.

"That's Max Garcia," Russell said. "He's the foreman, the number two guy for American Mining here in Encino. Nothing happens unless it goes through him or his boss, Boyce Hammond."

The truck pulled to the curb in front of the Jeep and I could see the nervousness on Saul's face. Garcia made no move to get out of his truck and I wasn't in the mood for a long wait or a stand-off just looking out a window. "Russell, thanks for the information. I might be back another time to talk some more."

"Love to have you back sometime, Jay. I used to get some overnight guests when American Mining sent their office people here once in awhile. I still keep a couple of rooms at the ready if you want to spend the night. Come early, we still get some folks in for happy hour and the beer is always cold just the way your father liked it."

We didn't know what to expect when we got outside but I stepped through the door and Saul followed closely behind. We walked straight to the Jeep and avoided eye contact with Garcia. That wasn't enough to keep him in his truck. He stepped out on to the street and walked toward us. He was a large man, tall and thick and covered with tattoos. Saul quickly got into the driver's seat and started the engine while I got in on the passenger side.

Garcia stood beside the Jeep, his expression anything but welcoming. "Who the hell are you guys? Why were you taking pictures at the mine?"

I wasn't interested in a conversation with the man. "Well, it's really none of your business but we're just doing a little sightseeing on our way to somewhere else."

"Look, smart ass, that mine is private property and you aren't welcome there. If I see you there again you'll have the kind of trouble you don't want." His look had turned from unwelcome to menacing.

Not surprisingly Saul couldn't stay silent. "We were on a public road not a private one. Better learn your fucking boundaries, pal."

"Listen here, asshole, around here there's no such thing as private or public, just American Mining. We say what goes and doesn't go. Got it?"

I wasn't surprised that Saul couldn't stay silent. "Wow, do you stand in front of a mirror and practice that tough guy routine?"

With that he threw the Jeep into gear and quickly pulled on to the street, forcing the man to jump out of the way. I looked back and saw him giving us the finger. We drove quickly up the hill and were surprised and relieved when the pick-up didn't follow us. A moment later we were over the crest of the hill and pulled into the Texaco station. Jack didn't greet us and I assumed he'd gone next door to the repair shop.

Saul stopped beside my car. "What the hell was all that? I thought we were doing a story about a dying little town and now we have some big goon giving us shit. My heart's still pounding."

I was as surprised as he was. "Something stinks here. There's a copper mine winding down its operations, no big deal, but that guy wants to go all top security on us. There must be something going on."

"Well we got a lot of video there and a ton of stills of every inch of the place. I also got some footage on the road into town, all those empty houses and the old motel, the kind of things we talked about. I don't think you'll need much more from me and I don't think I want to be around here after dark."

I could tell that my laid back photographer friend was more than just rattled, he was frightened. I tried to put him at ease. "Okay, thanks for spending the day here. I'm going to need more time to video some interviews with the locals, you know, telling the story from their point of view but I can get that later by myself. Let's just go back to our homes, have a drink and catch our breath. This might make more sense tomorrow. I'll call you in the morning."

Saul nodded. "Sounds good."

I reached into the back and grabbed my bag. Before I got out I put my hand on his shoulder. "Thanks again, man. Everything's cool." I said the words but wasn't sure if I believed them.

What Just Happened?

The drive back to Albuquerque was uneventful but I couldn't stop thinking about everything we had seen and heard in Encino. Between Russell's comments and Max Garcia's behavior all I could think was that the mine itself was at the center of my story. I just didn't know how yet. Katie was already home when I walked into the kitchen and as usual she could read me like a book.

"Geez, honey, you look like you're in a fog, what's wrong? Did something happen?"

I laid my bag on the counter and dropped on to a stool. "I'm not sure, maybe something, maybe nothing. I don't know."

"Well thanks for clearing that up."

"I'm sorry. It's just been a very strange and unexpected kind of day. What I thought would be an interesting little story about a dusty, little town on the verge of disappearing into history is more than that. It seems like that dusty, little town has a few secrets, or someone does."

"This sounds like a wine conversation." She pulled a bottle of Chardonnay from the refrigerator and while she opened it I talked.

"I've been there a couple of times now and talked to a few people. That and the little bit I found online didn't give me much information. That changed today. Saul and I had planned on a day of videos and photography and maybe talking to some more people and we got all of that and a lot more."

She handed me a glass. "What's a lot more?"

"We were up on a hill overlooking the mine and Saul got some great footage. But we both noticed that something didn't look right. Remember when I said the town looks like the people just got up and left? That's the way the mine looks too, like when a shift ended the miners just got into their cars and went home and never came back."

Well, didn't you say that somebody there told you there was no copper left to mine?"

"Yeah, that's what I was told. And it's like we talked about the other night when we were looking at Dad's photos, that happened two years ago but there are still some guys there. No sign of work going on in the pit but men and trucks still on the site. When a guy saw us with cameras he got into his pickup and came after us."

"What the hell! Was there any trouble?"

"Not really. He followed us to the hotel where we'd stopped. It's where those pictures of Dad were taken. The guy just drove past so we talked to the hotel owner awhile and then when we went back out to the Jeep the guy in the pickup was there waiting."

"Oh my God, what happened?"

"The guy, his name is Max, got out of his truck and came over to us and said we were trespassing at the mine and that we weren't welcome. Saul told him the road we were on was a public road. Of course being Saul he couldn't just leave it at that. He made a snide remark about the man's tough guy act and then we took off and didn't give him a chance to say anything more."

"It sounds like this story of yours could lead to trouble. Maybe you should get out of it."

"Don't worry, I'll be careful but Saul might not even go back when I do. Remember what happened on the Indian relics story? As soon as we found out that some of the relics might have been stolen by a professional antiquities ring Saul got nervous and bailed on me. He gets squeamish at the thought of trouble."

Katie pulled up the stool beside mine. "Well, don't be a hero for the sake of a story. And speaking of that, I was talking to a woman at the hospital about your project. Her brother used to work at a mine in Nevada and he told her when a mine closes down there has to be all kinds of things done. It's called decommissioning and they have to put the land back in order and do all kinds of environmental work. It sounded like a really big deal."

"That's what we were told too but from what we saw today none of that kind of work has been done. None. It's still this huge open pit of dirt and dust and rocks, nothing else. Two whole years of nothing happening." I reached into my bag and took out my laptop. "I'm going to Google *Mine Decommissioning* and see what it says."

Normally Katie didn't get overly involved in my work but I could tell she was worried about me. "Maybe you won't have to do that. If you want to find out more I can talk to that woman again and get her brother's number, he's living back here now. He could probably tell you a lot about what you saw and what should be happening there."

"Great idea. Maybe I can talk or even meet with him tomorrow. I need to start putting a story outline together and it would work better if I got some info from him first. I still want to search some stuff online though."

"Hold off on that for a bit, at least for tonight. Let's go out for a bite and a drink someplace. I can tell you're really wound up in this story already and you need to chill out for a while." She leaned over and kissed me. "You have a tendency to get up to your neck in the details. Take a break."

A couple of hours of good food and better wine were a big help in improving my mood. Crawling into bed was easy but falling asleep wasn't. As usual my mind went into full playback mode and I relived every minute of my day in Encino; the conversations with the town's sad holdouts, the strange situation at a supposedly idle mine and the unexpected altercation with Max Garcia. The more I thought about it all the more confused I became. And I knew the only way the answers would come would be from me going after them myself.

Searching for Something...
Anything

Despite my almost sleepless night I was at my desk early the next morning. I searched several internet sites on the mining industry and looked through a cache of still photos that Saul had already edited and emailed to me in advance of the video. With Katie's help I got the phone number of the man who worked at the Nevada mine. After a little bit of verbal arm twisting I talked him into meeting me for lunch, his choice and my treat. It might have been the best money I'd ever spent. The man, Billy Pickett, looked like he'd spent his entire life in the sun and wind. He'd been in mining for over twenty years and seemed to know the ins and outs of everything that happened in the pit and in the office.

We talked and ate our lunch and he was agreeable to letting me record our conversation. His knowledge of the decommissioning process was impressive and when we'd finished eating and our server had cleared our table I took out the stack of my father's photos. Billy looked at them carefully and pointed out a couple of things only a miner would know. But it was when I took out my phone and asked him to scroll through Saul's new photos that things really got interesting. He scrolled through a few of them then looked down at the ones spread on the table. He looked on the back of one of my Dad's photos, saw the date and then saw that the ones on my phone were sent just hours before we sat down. He looked up at me, shaking his head. "Holy shit, these were taken two years apart? What the hell has American been doin' up there, just sittin' on their asses?"

I was expecting that reaction. "That's why I wanted to talk to you. I'm no mining expert but even I can tell something smells funny here."

"You got that right. From what I see in these pictures there's still plenty of ore to dig. There's room for at least another six or eight benches. That's years of diggin'. They must have stopped for another reason."

"What other reason would a big outfit like American need to shut things down?"

Billy leaned back, still staring at the photos on my phone. "I just noticed somethin' here." He pointed to one of the photos on the table. See in that shot there, you can see three ore processin' tanks at the unloadin' area up top. That's where they dump the crushed ore into the chemical bath for extraction. But in the shot you and your friend took yesterday you can see that one of the tanks was moved over to the flat area by the shaft in the cliff." He pointed my phone screen toward me.

I studied it for a moment. "So if I understand what you just said, that tank was moved to the shaft area after the shutdown, after they stopped digging in the pit."

"Well, at least after they stopped diggin' for copper."

"What else would they be digging for in a copper mine?"

Billy smiled. "Copper is never alone down there in the ground. There's usually all kinds of other minerals mixed in and one of them is silver. We had some in the mine I was workin' at in Nevada. Not much but some, but you never really know how much will turn up." He scrolled to a particular photo on my phone and showed it to me. "As far as your story is concerned this is your money shot right here." He handed me the phone and as I studied the photo he said, "Your story isn't in the pit, it's in that shaft."

"You mean there's silver there, where the tank and all the trucks are sitting?"

"That'd be my guess. I figure they found a vein, maybe a big one and they wanted to keep it quiet, you know, away from the couple hundred guys in the pit."

"So if those guys in the pit went away they could concentrate on the silver."

"Exactly, with no one around to ask questions. I don't mean to sound suspicious but it's just a hunch and I think it's a good one." He tapped the photo on my phone and said, "It's a pain in the ass to move those tanks around, lots of time and overhead. You don't just do it without a damn good reason. On top of that they put it too far from the pit to be of any use day to day there."

"And a big vein of silver sounds like a great reason to move it." Things were starting to make sense to me except for one thing. "Okay, what about the decommissioning? That's required by law but there are no signs of it happening on-site."

"Yeah, that's kind of strange. I was part of decommissionin' crews on my last two sites. Once the company pulled the permit the clock started tickin' and we had to meet a deadline or pay penalties. Not big ones, just the slap-on-the-wrist kind, but we knew the boss was watchin' so we got it done."

"So American Mining shuts this place down and files the paperwork for a decommissioning. Assuming that's what they did why isn't it happening?"

"Hard to say. It could be a paperwork thing, you know, with the State or the EPA."

"Would that drag out for two years?"

"No, I doubt that. But American could have asked for an extension, you know, to kind of slow things down awhile. It happens all the time. Technically they could ask for more than one if they were good enough with the bullshit answers they'd have to give."

I leaned back and paused, trying to grasp everything Billy had deciphered from the photos. Finally I said, "Man, I'm so glad we had this talk. It looks like my story is still a mystery but it's one I think I understand now."

Billy smiled. "Glad I could help but you're a writer not a detective and this whole thing sounds, oh, how can I put this? It sounds like it could be kind of risky, maybe even dangerous. Just watch your back."

The list of small New Mexico towns I'd visited was about to grow. As I entered Estancia I couldn't help but notice the similarities to Encino. There was a main street with a compact business district and small, stucco homes on every surrounding block. The big difference was that Estancia was still alive and vibrant with people out and about and living normal lives. It was the county seat for Torrance County so if I wanted to dig for information on what was going on somewhere else in the county the Estancia courthouse was the place to start. I'd compiled a rough outline of what I thought were the main question marks of my story. My hours on Google and other online search engines had provided me with nothing but dry, statistical kinds of information like census counts, voter registration numbers and real estate values. It was helpful stuff but didn't begin to tell the people side of things.

Building signage led me to the Records office and I waited a few minutes while the lone female employee behind the counter finished up helping a man. She finally beckoned to me.

"Good morning," I began. "I'm looking for some information on several things over in Encino. I have them written down here."

As I flipped through my notebook the woman smirked and said, "It's been a long time since I heard anything about that place. It's like it dried up and blew away." Her smile and snarky tone on the subject were a huge contrast with the sadness in the voices coming from Encino. It pissed me off a little but I was careful with my tone.

"I need some information about the mine, about when they shut down."

"That's all done at the state and federal level. The best I can show you are photocopies of whatever paperwork was photocopied and filed with us."

"That'll work just fine."

The length of my wait time wasn't unexpected given the minimal staffing of a small town government operation but the woman finally returned and laid a file folder on the counter. "This is everything we have on the shutdown. You can look through it all and I can make you copies for a buck apiece."

She went into a back office while I pored through the stack of papers. An hour and a half and twenty-three dollars got me copies of the original decommissioning application, the first permit and two applications for extensions for completing the work. With that and some correspondence that gave me the names of the American Mining employees involved, I had a lot to read and digest when I got home. I'd also found a trove of old newspaper articles about the town. My cellphone camera worked great on getting shots of the yellowed pages and old photos of life back in the day. It was information that could fill in a lot of blanks but I had a feeling that my story still required more face time in Encino. I wasn't sure how I felt about that.

A Reluctant Return

That morning when I'd told Katie that I had to go back to Encino she wasn't happy about it. Up to that point my writing career had been more scholarly investigation than physical risk. Now it looked as though my new project had the potential to change that. When she asked me again why I had to go all I could say was, "It's what I do." Earlier in the morning I'd talked to a producer at the *History Channel* to update him on where I stood with my story research. I made sure to tell him about the run-in with Garcia and my suspicions about the mine. He seemed to have a good read on the situation and before we hung up he said, "Be careful." Now as I sat there waiting for Saul to answer his phone it was hard not to think about what I might be getting myself into.

"Hey, good morning, Jay, I figured I'd be hearing from you sooner or later, especially after what happened."

"What do you mean?"

"I mean I figured our little run-in with that thug in Encino probably rattled you the same way it did me."

My mild-mannered friend's comment didn't exactly surprise me. "Well, I admit the guy's reaction took me by surprise but I have a story to write here. You know the old saying, "you have to go where the story takes you" and this one's taking me back to Encino."

Saul was silent for a moment then said, "We have all kinds of photos and video, from ground level and the air, and you've talked to the locals.

"Yeah, but I didn't get them on audio and, even better, I'd like to get them on video.

What more is there to the story?"

I was glad he asked. "Well, I had a very interesting talk with a guy, a miner who knows all about the way things run, or are supposed to run. I showed him our photos and the ones my Dad took and he saw something. He said we've been looking for the story in the wrong place."

"You mean we shouldn't look in Encino?"

"No, he meant we were looking at the wrong things in the photos. Remember that shaft in the side of the hill? He has a hunch they found silver there, like maybe a whole lot of it and they want to keep it a secret."

Again Saul was quiet for a moment before he replied, "Well, that kind of fits with what happened when we were there. The guy with binoculars watching the rim, the big guy in the pick-up and the way he acted in front of the hotel. It all kind of fits."

"Yeah, and add to that the very sudden lay-off of a couple hundred guys working in the pit. My new miner friend said it looked to him like there's still plenty of copper left down there."

I could hear a long sigh and a moan from Saul. "So you said the story's taking you back to Encino but what's that have to do with me? I took video of every inch of that damn place, including the mine."

"I know, but we didn't really pay much attention to that shaft. It's just kind of been in the background and somehow we have to make it center stage. We have to try and see what's going on there.'"

"Come on, man, we're doing this for the *History Channel*. This isn't *CSI: Encino!*"

I was glad Saul couldn't see my smile because I wanted to keep things on a serious path. "I know but remember, we do documentaries and we have to document what the facts are. Without that we're just making crap and I don't want my name on crap."

Another long sigh and then, "I'm not going to be able to talk you out of this, am I?"

"Saul, I know we're in a situation we've never been in before. Maybe we're letting our imaginations get the best of us or maybe it's something real. But we've got time invested in this and we have to finish what we started."

Saul's silence made it clear that he was struggling with a decision. "So, what do you think?" I asked. "Are you in?"

"Shit, I guess so, but with conditions."

"Such as?"

"One, we find a different vantage point, a hidden one, not like that spot on the rim where they could see us.'

"Fair enough, what else?"

"No stopping in town. We don't know who'll see us and start talking. We meet someplace on the outskirts and take a back road up to the mine. I know a guy who hunts around there and he has some pretty good maps of the roads and trails."

"Okay, is that it?"

"One last thing." He paused. "If we run into that big guy again or anyone else who looks like trouble we get the hell out immediately and I'm done with the project."

Saul was a colleague and a friend and there was no way I could argue when I knew how strongly he felt. "Okay, deal."

Katie was very quiet and clearly troubled the next morning. We'd had a long conversation the night before, a conversation that drifted in and out of being an argument. She was worried about my chances for another confrontation with Garcia and I was too. I tried to assure her that Saul and I had everything carefully planned out and there'd be no chance for contact with anyone connected to the mine. We'd stay out of sight from the mine itself and not go into town. It would be a quick photo-shoot and then we'd leave. Not surprisingly she was unconvinced and I had to admit I was too, but of course I didn't say that.

On a quick call from the car I'd agreed to meet Saul at a rest stop on Route 54 east of Vaughn. It was far enough from Encino and the mine that no one could connect us to anything. He said he had worked out a route of backroads and trails that would take us to the east edge of the mine in a wooded area where we wouldn't be seen. It was already feeling like a scene from an old Western movie; riding through the high desert and sneaking up on the bad guys. I had to admit I was starting to feel a certain sense of adventure. It might even become an interesting part of the documentary. It could also be the beginning of something else.

Saul was waiting at the rest stop and his attire took me by surprise. He was dressed head to toe in full-on camo including a broad-brimmed hat covered with leaves and twigs. As I walked toward his Jeep I couldn't resist. I smiled and said, "Good morning, Rambo." He had a sheepish look and said, "Hey, make fun if you want to but we have to be invisible when we do this." He reached into the back seat and pulled out a camouflage shirt and cap. "These are for you."

There was no one else at the rest stop so I indulged his role-playing idea and changed into the shirt. I locked my car and we started the drive through the backroads and pinon forests. He'd estimated it was about three miles to the edge of the mine property and another hundred yards or so through the trees to the rim of the pit. By the time we'd come to a stop my entire body felt like it had been bouncing in a rock tumbler. We unpacked the camera equipment and some water and headed west on foot. The map turned out to be surprisingly accurate and when we'd finally reached the thicket of brush and mesquite we were looking out over the pit.

This part of the project was Saul's and I just followed his instructions on setting up the tripod and clearing a small opening in the branches so he'd be able to get a clear view of things. He took out his digital camera and attached the biggest telephoto lens I'd ever seen. He called it *The Truth Teller* because he could be so far away and still capture images of people who believed they were totally alone and unseen. The little smile on his face told me that my Rambo reference had been at least somewhat appropriate. When the tripod was ready and the camera was attached I draped a canvas cover over it all to hide any possible reflections from the sun. Saul adjusted the camera while I peered through the binoculars. We could see across the pit from a new angle with a clear, open view of the tunnel. There were three white trucks parked near the tank but no signs of people or activity. So we waited.

About ten minutes later a man stepped out of the office shack and met another man walking out of the tunnel. I heard Saul's camera shutter clicking while I watched. We had figured there'd be a lot of down time just watching the dust swirling and birds flying with not much to see from the mine but that didn't seem to happen. The two men were immediately joined by a third and moments later a large white box truck pulled into view. One of the men walked to the driver's door and then we saw the truck turn around and back into the area in front of the tunnel. They opened the rear doors of the box which, unfortunately, partially obscured the view of the tunnel. I turned to Saul. "Shit, I hope we didn't come all this way for nothing."

A few minutes later we saw a partial view of a forklift carrying a large wooden crate. It disappeared behind the truck then came into view again when it backed away empty. Saul took a few photos and said, "I wonder what they're loading. That truck isn't big enough to carry ore." Over the next hour we saw the forklift unload several more crates and with each one we noticed that the truck sat a little lower. Whatever was in the crates was very heavy. When a fourth crate was in place a man closed the truck doors.

After a few minutes of conversation the driver climbed back into the cab and slowly drove back down the entrance road. I wasn't sure what we had witnessed but whatever it was it seemed important enough for one of the men to take out binoculars and scan the ridge just like the time when we'd been spotted. He turned and looked in our direction then turned back toward the entrance road. We knew he hadn't seen us and Saul couldn't resist saying with a snarky smile, "Rambo, my ass."

On the way back to the rest stop we speculated as to what had been loaded on the truck and the only logical answer we could come up with was silver, probably in some refined form. We had no way of knowing how many other truckloads had left the mine since it had closed but there was no doubting that the value must be huge. After my meeting with Billy Pickett I was curious about the current going price and had checked it online. Even one truckload of silver at $21.45 an ounce would be a small fortune and it appeared that the operation had been going on for two years. The total haul must have been a staggering amount.

Back at the rest stop we sat in the Jeep and talked about the next steps to complete the documentary. It wasn't a very long conversation. Saul took off his hat, pulled back his hair and said, "Well, I can't think of any more stuff you'll need from me. We have stills and videos of the town and a shitload of stills of the mine. And now we have even more. Unless I'm missing something, with your copy you've got hours of images to dig through and edit."

I took off the camo shirt and cap and tossed them on to the backseat. "Yeah, I think you're right. I still need interviews with the town folks and I'll use my little video camera for that. I'll send my outline and videos to the guys at the *History Channel* and a bunch of your stuff too. They can check things out and hopefully they'll give me a Notice to Proceed letter."

We sat in silence for a moment, both of us aware that we were side-stepping the obvious. Finally Saul asked, "So how are you going to tie this silver operation into the story of the dying town?"

That question had been gnawing at me ever since Billy Pickett brought it up. I looked at Saul and said, "I don't have that worked out yet. Stay tuned."

The drive back to Albuquerque was a blur and my head was filled with the documentary. I knew that getting photos of men loading crates into a truck proved nothing. Adding that to the suspicious behavior of the men still didn't make a story. Billy Pickett's theory seemed to tie it all together but it still wasn't enough. There had to be someone in Encino that knew about the truck and whether there had been others. My return trip to the town would have to include some more probing into the mine and the men who were running it. I hoped there'd be a way to do it discretely... and safely.

Just like she was with that day's photoshoot with Saul, Katie wasn't happy about me making another return to Encino. She was glad we'd been able to get our shots and get out cleanly but she knew as well as I did the next visit wouldn't be the same. In hindsight I regretted mentioning the mysterious truck loading at the mine. After dinner I sat in my office going through my notes and scribbling a loose outline of the next day's tasks. She came in with the usual glasses of after-dinner wine and sat down. As she handed me my glass I could read her mood so I started the conversation. "Babe, we're in the home stretch on this one. Just a few video interviews with the local folks and I'll be back on the road home.

"I wish I could believe that but I can't, not with everything you've told me, Billy Pickett's suspicions, the guy with the binoculars, the other guy who got in your face and now they're loading something into a truck at a mine that's supposed to be closed. I don't like the idea of you getting caught in the middle of something. That's not supposed to be part of what you do."

"I'm a documentary writer and I'm supposed to go where the story takes me."

"That's a bumper sticker not a strategy."

Sometimes it's obvious when a disagreement has no clear resolution and this was one of them. The documentary was close to being finished. It would be a story about people and a small American town turned upside down. The mystery of the silver and the mine closing didn't have to be resolved to tell the story. That was my only argument for going back to Encino but it wasn't enough to convince Katie. It was a quiet night after that and an even quieter morning when I left for my return visit.

The People Speak

Even though I'd only discovered Encino a few weeks earlier I had already developed an affection for the place. It was mostly because of the people. The stories my father had told me and the photos he'd taken painted a picture of an idyllic American town. What I'd experienced in person were just the remnants of it. The narrative of the documentary was coming together and I had a pretty well developed outline. It would open with a brief introduction and history of Encino, the basic facts and figures of life before the mine opened.

My trip to the courthouse and my online searches had given me a lot of background on American Mining and the history of the Encino operation. Those were the golden years of the town. Details of the mine closing helped me form a timeline of the slow, painful withering away of day to day life there. What was left would be the hard, emotional part of the story. I was going to get some of the locals to tell me the before and after of their lives in their own words and on video. I wasn't looking forward to it but I knew it would be the heart and soul of the story.

During my drive I'd mentally rehearsed the list of questions I'd put together for the interviews but the more I rehearsed the more I knew that approach would be too stiff and contrived. These were good people who'd had their lives changed in ways they never imagined. I decided to just sit with them and talk, let them tell me what they'd experienced and how they felt in their own words. They would write the script for me.

When I pulled into the Texaco station I saw Jack walking toward me from the repair shop. He looked just as worn down as he had the times I'd seen him before but when he saw me he managed a slight smile. I took it as a compliment.

"You back again, Mr. Rorbach?"

I nodded. "Yeah, I'm back, Jack, but this time it's kind of work-related. My work."

"I never knew what it is you do for a livin'," he said.

"I'm a writer. I write documentaries, historical documentaries for TV. I just finished one about stolen Indian artifacts."

Jack looked puzzled. "So what are you writin' about here? There's not much to say about this place."

"Well, Jack, I disagree. Between the things my father told me about Encino and things I've learned I think there's a story here, a good story." I waited a moment then added, "I was hoping I could interview you about your life here, about all the changes and the things you've gone through."

He tilted his head as if he was studying me. "Me, I'm just a pump jockey."

"Jack, you're a lot more than that. You grew up here. Your family is from here. You've seen and lived through all the good and bad stuff. I'd really like to hear about it."

He shrugged. "Well, I guess I can talk to you awhile if you really think it'll be worth somethin'. Let's go inside."

It took me a few minutes to decide on the best setting for the shoot and where to set up the video camera. Jack looked nervous and I noticed him brushing back his hair and straightening his shirt collar. With the camera resting on the cash counter and Jack sitting in a squeaky, old stool behind it, we began our conversation. I followed a basic format of simple questions about his life in Encino but mostly just let him talk. He rambled a bit but his words were authentic and heartfelt. A few of his comments hit me hard and I knew they'd give the story an emotional edge. Comments like, "I grew up here, never thought of leavin' until everyone else did. Now I think about how I've got no place to go and I'm so damn tired of sayin' goodbye to people." And, "Sometimes I get so angry I just want to punch something." Another one was, "I know I drink too much but I've got lots of time to do it and no reason to stop." And he said something that he seemed to struggle getting out, "I used to be big in this town, the police chief, a business man, an elder in the church. Now the town's gone and so is everythin' I used to be." He stopped and I knew the pain on his face could be the centerpiece of the story.

While I was packing up my camera I asked him, "Hey, one last thing. Have you seen a large, white box truck driving in the area lately?"

"Yeah, it's from the mine. I've seen it drive by four or five times on the way out of town, but it might have passed by other times when I wasn't here. Of course they just keep movin', never stop to give me a little business."

"Any idea where they might have been headed?"

"Nope, there's lots of places south of here but I saw it had Mexico plates so it's anybody's guess where it ends up."

I had him top off my tank and we shook hands. He asked me who else I was going to talk to for the documentary. I told him Rita was next and then I was going to get more video of the town and surrounding area. I'd end the trip late afternoon with a visit to The Bond so I could interview Russell. His eyes widened but he didn't say anything more.

Half an hour later I was doing my interview with Rita. Like Jack she was a little nervous but cooperative and willing to talk. And like Jack she offered several moving comments. One was, "I'm so tired of all the driving, to Vaughn, to Clines Corners, to so many other places like Encino used to be. For groceries I drive. For my prescriptions I drive. Even for the damn doctor I drive." Her sadness really showed when she said, "My husband's long gone. I know I'm gonna die here all alone. I try not to think about that too much."

My trek through town was slow and I did a lot of it on foot. I only saw a few people and I made no attempt to do anything but wave to them. By four o'clock I pulled up to The Bond. It seemed like a good time to text Katie that I was nearly finished in Encino, all was well and I'd be back on the road home soon. I hoped that would ease some of her worries.

After I checked my email I, grabbed my stuff and stepped out. I was only a few steps from the door when it opened and I saw Russell. "Hey, Mr. Rorbach, glad to see you again!" He stepped out on to the sidewalk and we shook hands. "I looked at the broom in his hand and he said, "Time for my daily sweeping of the front entrance. The damned dust never stops, even without the mine. My wife used to do it twice a day, well, before she left." He looked at my camera bag and asked, "What's all this, you want to take pictures of the place?"

"Well, first of all, it's about time you called me Jay. I'm finishing up a documentary about Encino, it's for television, and after I visited The Bond and met you on my last trip I thought it would make a great part of the story. I'd like to hear what you have to say about things around here too."."

He smiled. "Well, I'm flattered. Let me finish up here. How about you pull your car down the alley here and take one of the covered spots in the back. There's a rear entrance and I'll meet you there."

A few minutes later he was holding the rear door open and I was carrying my video camera and notes through the door. It struck me that even that part of The Bond had been meticulously maintained. We walked down a hallway that by-passed the bar room and connected to the front lobby. I looked around and said, "You know, Russell, I think the bar room would be the perfect place to do this." I was thinking of my father when I said it.

"That's fine with me. The bar's always kind of been the center of things around here. I have to do a few things there anyhow, to get ready for the late afternoon beer drinkers." He smiled and added, "I've got the only cold, draft beer in the whole damn town."

He went about his task of checking the taps and kegs while I set up the video camera. When we were ready I said, "Okay, stand there in front of that beautiful back bar, relax and let's talk."

I followed the same process as I had earlier, asking a few questions but mostly letting him express himself in his own way and in his own words. Russell was a talkative guy and I got a lot more conversation than I would need. That included a couple of emotional comments like, "Everyone who's still here knows everyone else who's still here. We know we're all stuck here together." He made another comment that I knew must have been shared by the people who had left; "Some of us were really upset when they closed the Catholic church. It was where we all gathered. A few of us, me included, didn't go all in for the religious stuff, you know, God and all that. To us it was just a place to be around other folks." There was a long pause and then, "Now it's like God left too and just forgot about us, about Encino." There were tears in his eyes.

When I had what I needed and sensed that Russell had spoken his peace we wrapped things up. While I was packing my camera he said, "Go ahead and stash your camera in your car then come on back in. I'll pour you a cold one on the house."

It wouldn't be the first time I'd driven home with a beer or two in me. "Sounds good. I'll be right back."

It only took me a few minutes to put my things in the trunk and lock the car and when I got back to the bar room Russell had already poured. I sat down on a stool and he slid the mug toward me. "Here you go, Jay, this was your father's favorite."

While he set out a small line of mugs we talked about my project. I told him about my other interviews and all of the video we had shot from the drone. His only comment was, "I just hope whoever sees your show will understand what happened here, what happened to us."

We were interrupted by noise from the front door. Two men came in and walked over to the end of the bar. They glanced at me but showed no interest. From their clothing I could tell they worked at the mine and I suddenly wondered if I should leave. I decided to stay until I'd finished my Dad's favorite beer. "Hey, Russell, can you point me toward the Men's Room?"

"Sure, through that arch and on the left." He grinned. "We put it close to the bar for when the guys are in a hurry."

I didn't have to use the restroom but it gave me an opportunity to listen in on the men's conversation. I stood there with the door open a few inches and was able to hear them fairly well. Suddenly the writer in me came up with an idea. I took out my phone, set it on Video Record and put it into my shirt pocket so that even without an image I could at least record the sound. I stood there quietly and listened. One man said, "You know, this is kind of a celebration. In a few days we'll all be out of this shit hole town." I wondered if Russell had heard the insult.

The other man replied, "Yeah, Boyce double checked right before I left the shack. The truck is on its way. Tomorrow morning at eight o'clock we'll be loading it for the last time, then we all head south. Sunshine, beaches, tequila and a whole lot of money."

"Did he say how long it would take to convert everything into cash? I don't want to hang around there for long, I've got things to do back in Santa Fe."

"You mean that girl from the casino?"

I heard the front door again and a moment later a greeting. "Hey, Max, join the party."

The only person from the mine who'd ever laid eyes on me had just walked in. The way he acted at our first meeting was scary enough and I felt trapped. All I could think about was getting out of that restroom and back to my car. I found a little comfort in the fact that my phone was still taking in the conversation. Whatever might happen there would at least be a recording of what was said and what might happen. I stood there another moment and listened.

I heard Max say, "I guess we can all afford to pick up the check tonight."

"Yeah, especially you. Your piece of the pie is a lot bigger than ours."

Max laughed. "But every piece of that big, silver pie tastes delicious. And remember, nobody gets a bite until everything is there, unloaded, checked out and on its way."

"I'll be glad when we can stop lookin' over our shoulder."

"Yeah, me too. Boyce said we gotta get that last truck loaded and on the road. He says corporate's getting a little too curious about what's goin' on around here."

I wondered where Russell was and if he was listening. I couldn't stay in the Men's Room much longer. Men who drink beer have to get rid of it eventually. I knew I'd have to deal with Max and when I did I wanted it to be out in the open and not in a restroom. I took a deep breath and walked back into the bar room. I immediately caught Max's attention and he turned toward me. I'd never seen a grin quite so intimidating.

"Well, look here, boys, it's that guy I told you about, Mr. Binoculars."

They stood there staring and I kept walking. I made it back to my stool. Russel appeared from a store room behind the bar and walked over to me. He leaned toward me and said quietly, "Sorry, they usually don't stop in until later. Maybe you should head on out of here."

I had no clue what to do. The longer I stayed the better the chance of some kind of confrontation. All of the time I'd spent on the documentary got me what I needed, at least I hoped so. I had the *what* and the *how* of Encino's story. What I didn't yet have was the *why*. I wondered if that was even a part of things, if it really mattered.

Max Garcia interrupted my thoughts.: "Hey, Binocular Boy, I thought I made it clear you aren't welcome around here."

"This is my place, Max," Russell said sharply, "and he's my guest. Just settle down."

Garcia ignored him. "So who are you snooping on today? Where's your buddy with the Jeep?" His friends just stood in silence, watching.

Garcia was big enough to break me in half and I had a feeling he was halfway toward wanting to do just that. I really wanted to leave, drive home and try to finish the story of Encino. But at that moment, in that bar room I realized that the end of the story, the *why* of it all, was standing right in front of me, and leaving wasn't an option. As I swiveled toward Garcia I saw Russell walk back into the store room.

For the next fifteen minutes Garcia sat on his stool and I sat on mine. We exchanged glares mixed with occasional comments about his privacy and my rights. It seemed like a stalemate until another man came through the front door. Garcia turned toward him, grinned and said, "Hey, Boyce, good timing. We were celebrating when this guy here broke the mood. This is the guy with the binoculars from last week."

Boyce Hammond was clearly the man in charge. He didn't have the sun baked, calloused look of the others. He looked like a man who gave orders and watched men follow them. I took an instant disliking to him.

Russell came out from the storeroom and tried to break the tension. "What'll you have, Boyce, your usual?"

Hammond looked at him and nodded then turned his attention back to me. "There are all kinds of places a man can stop for a drink, places that aren't in this shitty little town. But you decided to stop here. Why?"

I honestly thought if Hammond and I had been the only ones in the room I would have gotten off my stool, stood nose to nose with him and told him to go fuck himself. But the very large Max Garcia and his two almost as large friends were a very real part of the situation. If things turned south I'd be on the bloody and battered side of a brawl. My only defense was they didn't know that I knew about their operation and I had to try to keep them guessing and use it as leverage if I needed to.

I tried to look calm and confident as I took a sip of my beer and turned toward Russell. "This is great beer. No wonder my father liked it." Hammond and his bunch looked at each other, seeming to be disappointed that I wasn't shaking in my shoes. I turned back to Hammond. "This isn't a shitty little town. It's a nice little town with nice people in it. It's too bad that most of them had to leave a nice place like this for no good reason."

I sensed that I'd caught Hammond off-guard. "What in the hell does that mean?"

I took another long, slow sip of beer. "Mmm, so good." Facing Hammond again I continued, "I mean all those nice people lost their town, or should I say they had it taken away from them."

Garcia looked at me, gave a side-eye to Hammond and said, "You little shit. You don't know nothing about what goes on around here."

Hammond again asked, "So why did you stop here?"

"Trying hard to look relaxed and not ready to wet my pants, I answered, "I could ask you the same thing. You closed the mine, when was it, like two years ago? You could be drinking at some fine place in Denver yet here you are."

Garcia stood up. "Boyce, want me to send this guy on his way?"

I was surprised when Russell raised his voice and said, "Look, you guys, this is my bar, my place. I decide who drinks here!"

Hammond wouldn't let up. "So, when you were looking over the mine with those binoculars and being where you shouldn't have been, what were you looking for?"

"Nothing in particular. I never saw an open pit mine before and I was kind of curious, that's all."

"Curiosity can get people in trouble. What did you see? Was that the only day you were snooping around?"

It was obvious that Hammond and his crew were nervous. It sounded like their two year-long silver scheme was almost finished and all of a sudden some stranger shows up in the middle of their little wrap party. I took the last sip of my beer and stood up. "Russell, thanks for the beer. I hope to see you again sometime." I'd only taken two steps when Garcia strode toward me and blocked my path to the hallway.

"You aren't leaving until Mr. Hammond says you can leave."

"Knock it off!" Russell shouted. "Let him go."

Garcia grinned. "Mr. Hammond's in charge here."

A voice from the front door said, "Nope, I am." It was Jack and when I saw him all I could do was stare. He was standing tall and erect, no slouching at all, dressed in his police chief uniform from his Stetson down to his boots. A holstered 9mm pistol hung on his right hip. His expression shouted confidence. The room was silent as if everyone was waiting for him to say something. He seemed to be enjoying the stares and I detected a slight smirk just before he asked, "Is there a problem here?"

The miners looked at each other and then Hammond took a step toward Jack. "What's with the uniform, Jack? You don't have any authority here."

"I was appointed Chief of Police on April 17, 2008. I never resigned, retired or got fired."

Hammond grinned. "The town is finished and you know it. There's no one here to pay you and yet somehow you think you're still in charge?"

Jack nodded, rested his hand on the handle of his gun and said, "Yes, I do."

Russell shrugged. He stepped forward, leaned on the bar and said, "How about we just call it a day. You boys settle your tab and head on out of here."

Garcia snarled, "We'll leave when we're ready to leave."

Jack walked up to Hammond and stopped just a few feet in front of him. He glared at Garcia then looked back at Hammond, almost nose to nose and said, "I think you're ready."

Garcia walked up to Jack. "If you weren't carrying that pistol I'd kick your ass."

Jack's eyes never left Garcia as he slowly reached down, pulled his handgun from the holster and brought it crashing down on the big man's head. Garcia groaned and crumpled to the floor.

No one moved or said a word for a few moments but then Hammond looked down at Garcia. "Guys, help Max get to his feet and let's get the hell out of here. Big day tomorrow and all that."

Hammond looked warily at Jack then took out his wallet, laid a hundred dollar bill on the bar and said to Russell, "Keep the change, it looks like you'll need it."

Jack followed the group to the door and waited outside to make sure they all left. When he walked back into the bar he said, "Good thing you called me, Russ. That could have gotten out of hand real quick."

Russell was smiling and shaking his head.

It was starting to get dark out and I wanted to get back on the road to Albuquerque as soon as I could but I knew there was something we had to talk about. I looked at Russell, "When I was in the restroom I overheard those guys talking about something and I recorded part of it." I took my phone from my shirt pocket and played back the audio. Did you hear it too?"

Russell nodded. "I think so, something about loading the last truck in the morning and never having to come back to our shit hole town."

I was glad he'd heard them too. They all listened as I played the audio again. "Jack, it sounds like the same white box truck we talked about, the one with Mexico plates."

Jack looked back toward the front door then pulled a stool away from the bar and dropped into it. "The sound on your video was kind of fuzzy. What all did they say?"

"They were talking about how the truck was due at the mine at eight o'clock tomorrow morning. They're going to load it, they said for the last time, and that it was heading south. They talked about beaches and money and margaritas so it sure as hell sounds like it's going to Mexico."

Russell chimed in, "And the one guy was wondering how long it would take to convert the silver into cash.'

Jack sat silently for a moment then nodded. "Russ, I think you better lock up for the night and head home in case one of them gets nervous and comes back. Mr. Rorbach...Jay, I think you better get back on the road home now. I have some calls to make, the sooner the better."

"What are you going to do...Chief?" Russell asked.

Jack stood up, straight and tall, and said, "I'm goin' to make sure things are ready for eight o'clock tomorrow morning."

I didn't know what he had planned but I knew, whatever it was, there was no way I could help him even though I wanted to.

Jack handed me his official Police Chief business card and said. "I might be needin' you to come back and talk some more, and bring your pictures with you. Maybe your friend in the Jeep, Saul., bring him too."

The three of us exchanged handshakes and a few minutes later I was headed out of Encino toward Route 60, keeping an eye on my rearview mirror the whole time. What had seemed back in the bar to be the end of my story was feeling like something else. I got on to I-40 and the closer I got to home the more it felt like the final scene of my documentary was still up in the air.

My late dinner with Katie seemed almost celebratory. The trips through central New Mexico, the photos and videos and the small mountain of information I'd gathered could now be turned into my documentary; a fascinating and moving story of the demise of a small town, or at least most of the story. We kicked a bottle of Zinfandel and I smiled a lot but I kept my concerns hidden. I couldn't stop wishing I could be back in Encino at eight o'clock the next morning.

Encino Redux?

My working relationship with Saul usually had me in the lead, writing the storyline and setting the pace while Saul followed up on what I needed for the projects. I was surprised the next day when I got a very excited lunch-hour phone call from him. "Hey, man, are you watching the news? Turn on KOB, they're reporting from Encino, the mine!"

I got up and turned on the small flat-screen in my office and tuned in to the station. I kept the phone to my ear. A woman reporter was standing, microphone in hand, with the mine shack in the background. A chyron across the bottom of the screen read *Silver Theft Ring Uncovered.* "Holy shit, that's Encino, that's our mine!"

"I know, and check it out, there's the box truck we saw them loading."

We continued to watch the coverage as the camera scanned the vast pit. When the cameraman cut back to the reporter, Linda Ruiz, there was Jack standing beside her, in full uniform and standing tall. The chyron at the bottom of the screen read: *Jack Riley, Encino Police Chief.* It was clear to the camera that he was in charge. He calmly gave her a recap of the events of the previous evening and that morning; the altercation at The Bond that provided a hint of what was going to happen, the calls to the State Police and the surprising cooperation from American Mining. It was a big story for a small town cop. The proud, confident look on his face was the antithesis of the sad, hopeless look he usually carried with him. I felt happy for him.

Saul's excitement hadn't waned. "This is big stuff! I've been watching for a while and it sounds like this silver theft has been going on for a long time. They said even the FBI is involved."

"Yeah, it looks like Billy Pickett was right.

"So what do you think happens next, does this involve us somehow, like will they want to talk to us?"

"Oh, count on it. Russell and I overheard some stuff at the hotel and he's the one who called Jack…Chief Jack. He knows about our photos at the mine so I won't be surprised if we're asked to sit down with the cops too."

"The reporter said it's a possible federal crime. This is just crazy that we know so much about it. This is so cool!"

"Yeah, but let's just calm things down and see where it all goes from here."

For the next couple of days I did the only thing I could; I continued with the story as I knew it. A small town was dying and I was chronicling everything that had brought it to this point. I had mountains of information, interviews, photos and video. It was already a good story. I had the *what* and the *how* and it looked like I finally had the *why*. But as sensational as the headlines might have been I knew I had to keep my focus on the people.

Over the course of a few weeks I'd assembled a huge trove of images; everything from old back and white shots of the town over the years of its life to the new full color shots of what was left of the place. I storyboarded them on a wall in my office and wrote my dialogue by speaking it aloud as I looked at the photos. I felt like I was there walking the streets and talking to the good folks of Encino along the way.

My workdays were long but I made sure to set aside time to keep an eye on the ongoing story of the silver theft. It grew daily as the list of criminal charges expanded from Theft by Deception to Attempt to Defraud the Federal Government to Transporting of Stolen Property Across an International Boundary. Boyce Hammond, Max Garcia and their henchmen on-site weren't the only ones involved in the scheme. American Mining's Chief Engineer and their Chief Operating Officer were also implicated and charged. Tens of millions of dollars were enough of an enticement to drag those normally honest people over the line. Even the networks had picked up the story but they were handling as just another news event. Sady, the whole thing played out as a story where the American Mining stockholders were the victims of the scheme with no mention of the damage done to the citizens of Encino.

There was another part of the story that went mostly unnoticed amidst all of the drama of corporate greed and misconduct. It turned out that

Billy Pickett had been correct on another matter related to the story. The open-pit copper mine had not played out as was declared in the paperwork filed for the decommissioning. Like he'd suspected, that part had been a ruse to allow Hammond and his team to work in the shaft without a daily audience. They'd filed extensions to delay the land restoration simply to give them time to finish their theft. The truth was that there was plenty of copper left to extract and there was an unconfirmed report that American Mining was mulling over a plan to regroup and open the pit again. I had no idea if anyone in Encino knew anything about it and because an investigation was ongoing I'd decided not to include the theft in the final documentary.

When my story was close enough to being finished we still had three days left until deadline. Saul joined me for the final editing. My usually laid-back partner was quiet as we watched the interviews with the locals and I even noticed tears in his eyes when Jack's part came on. All he said the entire time was "Good stuff, man, good stuff." After a few minor tweaks and edits for time, we finished it. I broke out a bottle of twelve year-old bourbon and we sat back congratulating ourselves on a job well done. It was finally easy to laugh at everything we'd gone through to finish the project.

But something took the edge off my celebration, something that had been playing on my mind for a couple of weeks. I was afraid to bring it up to Saul. We'd just told a sad story of the near death of an American town. A story of good people forced to uproot their lives and move elsewhere against their will and with no warning. Yet the whole idea of Encino being dead still seemed unsettled. Given the situation It couldn't really be called a viable place to live but the bones were still there. Streets, buildings, infrastructure and even neighborhoods were still in place. It needed people to bring it back to life. I looked over at Saul. The look of satisfaction on his face was obvious and I didn't want to say anything that would change that. To him our project had been completed and was ready to hand over to *The History Channel*. Done. Finished. End of story. The business side of me agreed and I was ready to book my flight to Los Angeles to deliver the project. After they had a few weeks for tweaking and minor editing for time *Not Dead but Almost* would be ready to air. But a small, nagging voice kept telling me it was too soon to call it a wrap.

What's In It for Us?

A large, yellow van, with a cartoonish graphic that read *Southwest Ghosts,* pulled up in front of the abandoned motel around 9:30 on Wednesday morning. Jack was on a ladder changing the lightbulb over the entrance to his station so he had a clear view of things next door. He watched as five people got out and began roaming around the parking lot, phone cameras in hand and visibly excited about the old place. The sign by the edge of the road was badly weathered but the name *Encino Motel* was still readable. Three of the people posed for selfies in front of it. A young man in jeans tugged at the locked front door and tried to peer in through the dirty glass. Jack got down from the ladder and watched as a short, plump woman in a broad-brimmed hat and sunglasses walked across the parking lot toward him. She was carrying a notebook and writing in it as she walked. When she was within earshot she called out, "Good morning, do you have a minute?"

He nodded and waited for her to get closer, then answered, "Better tell your friends to be careful over there. That sign almost blew over in a storm last month and it's not safe to get too close to it."

She turned and looked at the activity for a moment then turned back toward Jack. "Oh, it's okay, they'll be careful. Listen, I'm Marnie Sassman. I'm the Field Supervisor for our tour company. We're looking at Encino as a possible addition to ghost town tours and my crew is with me to check things out." She stopped and turned back toward the motel. "Jason, keep trying to get that door open."

Jack stepped around her and shouted, "No, don't touch that door! All of you, get away from the buildin' and the sign and do it now! It's not safe."

Marnie was clearly caught off guard. She turned back toward her group. "Okay, everyone, just wait there quietly and I'll be back with you in a few minutes." When she turned to face Jack she could tell he wasn't pleased with her and the rest of her bunch. "I'm sorry, we didn't realize it was unsafe over there."

"So the big, red *CAUTION* sign wasn't a clue?" His voiced dripped with sarcasm.

She chose to ignore his comment and handed him her business card. "We saw the wonderful documentary about your town on *The History Channel* and we weren't aware that the place was so empty, so closed down looking. It just seemed like a natural fit for us. We run guided tours of ghost towns in this part of the state. Duran and Ancho are two of our most popular stops and we'd like to add Encino because it's close enough to be part of the same route. We call it the *Forgotten Places Tour* and people just love it."

To Jack, her callous idea and the excited smile that went with it were hard to stomach. He tried to be polite. "So what happens on your tours?"

Marnie's smile never faded as she laid out her sales pitch. "Well to start with, we would only do the tours on weekends, one on Saturday and one on Sunday. The van driver will call your contact person an hour or so before arrival. We ask that people stay off the streets to make the town look as empty and abandoned as possible. We also would suggest that you not repair or repaint anything. People want that old, faded look. It just adds to the whole ghost town experience."

It was all Jack could do to hold his temper in check. "How does it benefit the town, I mean like our businesses?"

"Well, we still have some details to work out like how long the tour would last and how much exploring we'd let our customers do, you know, walking around and so forth. But we'd need you to have restrooms available somewhere and maybe a place to purchase water, coffee and other beverages."

"What about your van, would you need gas for it?"

"Oh, probably not. We fill the tank before we leave Albuquerque, make the tour and then refill it in Clines Corners on the way back."

That was all Jack could handle. "So, to your company, Encino has been forgotten. It will just be a place to walk around and feel sorry for its people, maybe take a piss and then get back in the van and talk about us on the way back home. Well, lady, people still live here. It's our home, not part of a tourist jaunt. You can't expect us to hide in our houses so you all can pretend we're not really here."

Marnie was wide-eyed, her mouth hanging open. "I'm so sorry, sir, I meant no offense. We thought Encino would like the recognition of being part of our tour."

"Well you thought wrong," Jack growled. "Encino isn't dead so I suggest you all get back in your little van and find your ghost town somewhere else." He stood there, hands on his hips, and watched the rattled woman hurry back to the motel parking lot and gather her team. He couldn't hear their conversation but the way they were glaring at him said enough. Within a few minutes they were back on the road and out of sight. It took Jack most of the morning to calm down and put his anger behind him.

It had been two months since *Not Dead but Almost* was broadcast. Since Jack had been present for the show's entire research and interview process he knew exactly what was in it. It was a respectful examination of the demise of a small American town. No sugar coating or pretending, just an honest and emotional look at what had happened to Encino. The woman from the tour company had seen something totally different and he couldn't help but wonder how many other viewers had seen it the same way. Before the documentary, did anyone know about or care about Encino? And now what were they thinking?

He got his answers a few days later when a rental car pulled into the station. Two men who'd only introduced themselves as being from American Mining asked Jack to fill the tank and to give them directions to the mine. They didn't say much but as Jack pumped their gas they stared down the street. He heard them talking quietly about the downtown. They were just as quiet while Jack rang up the transaction but he understood why. How could they act normal and friendly with a man whose town they had all but killed?

After that visit happened a slow but steady stream of other American Mining people had come to town. Some looked like executives and others like men who'd spent their time outdoors in the pit. Jack tried to strike up conversations with them but got little more than small talk and a thank you. He had the feeling they'd all been coached on what to say and not say. A few of them spent a night or two at The Bond but he'd overheard other ones talking about their hotel accommodations in Albuquerque.

Apparently The Bond wasn't up to their standards except as a place for a beer before they left town.

After a few weeks of those visits and trying to figure out if they meant anything Jack thought it would be a good time to get a few of the locals together to share information. On a Tuesday in the late afternoon they gathered at The Bond. It was a fitting venue for a reappraisal of Encino's past, present and future. Between Jack's service station, Rita's café, Russell's hotel and Joe Theobald's ranch they made up a good cross section of the town's shrunken business community.

Russell walked over to the table and set a glass in front of Rita. "Since when have you been a martini drinker?" he asked. She grinned and answered, "Since before I was old enough to drink them legally. I have one every night at home."

He smiled and sat down. "Okay, now that everyone has a drink let's talk about what in the hell's going on up at the mine."

Joe started. "Well, since the main road in there goes over my land I guess I have a better look at things than ya'll do. First it was just a few SUVs but now there's a lot of truck traffic, pick-ups and light duty stuff, nothing real big."

"Yeah," Rita added, "they've been coming into the café for lunch. "Nice fellas but kind of quiet. I've picked up bits and pieces of their conversations but I'm not exactly sure what they're talking about."

"What kinds of bits and pieces?" Jack asked. "I've tried to listen in the same way when they stop by the station. When they think I'm listening they stop talking."

"Well, I hear things like, they want to move some kind of tanks in and one guy said next week they'll have three flatbeds on the way from somewhere. It makes no sense to me."

Russell sat back in his chair, beer in hand. "Flatbeds mean they're hauling something big and heavy, like some kind of equipment."

Jack nodded. "That makes sense with what I read in the Albuquerque paper this morning. American wouldn't confirm anything but the rumor is they want to reopen the pit, get it up and running again."

Joe shook his head. "That's just great. That means all that goddamned dust will be blowing my way again." He leaned back and scratched his unshaven chin. "Of course, that's something I guess I could get used to if I had to."

There was a long silence before Jack said, "You know, if there's any chance that things are goin' to get back up and runnin' it means people will be comin' back here, back to work.

Russell wasn't quite so optimistic. "Let's not jump the gun here. First of all, we don't know one damn thing for certain, just rumors. And even if it's all true, after the way they shut things down and sent all those people packing, don't be surprised if nobody trusts them enough to come back. Nobody wants to go through all that again."

Rita took a long sip of her martini. "But on the bright side, the banks are holding the paper on a lot of empty houses and I'm betting they'll let them go cheap. I've seen some folks going up and down the streets looking at them. She finished draining her glass and held it up for Russell to see. He walked over and took it from her. "Geez, Rita, that was quick." He saw the expression on her face and said, "Okay, I'll get you another one."

For the next hour the four friends, neighbors and business colleagues talked, drank, drank some more and tried to make sense of what was happening around them. They all agreed that the various options made for an unpredictable future. Those options ran from the embarrassment of being viewed as a ghost town to getting their lives back close to the way they once were. More than likely the answer would be somewhere in between. They'd also wondered aloud if there was anything they could do to control the outcome or if they'd just have to sit back and let others decide their fate. The consensus was best expressed when Jack declared, "American claims that they built this town. That's true to a point but so did a lot of small business people like us. American single-handedly tore it down and I don't think we should give them a chance to pretend they didn't. If there's goin' to be some kind of a revival of Encino we're goin' to be the ones who write the rules for it."

"So What's the Plan?"

When I pulled into the station Jack was watching for me from the doorway. Except for a phone call a few days prior, we hadn't talked since the documentary had been broadcast and as we walked toward each other it was hard to do anything but smile. "Jack, how the hell are you?

We shook hands and he answered, "Glad you could meet with me. I'm sure the last thing you expected was another long drive to Encino."

"Relax, it goes with the territory. Writers go to where the story is."

"Well, I'm not sure if you'll get a story out of this but like I told you in my message, there's shit load of stuff happenin' here and I think we need your help in comin' up with the right way to handle it."

"And the shit that's happening here is happening because of my documentary. From what you told me I'm not sure if that's a good thing or a bad thing."

"Neither are we. But since we don't have a Mayor or a Town Council anymore whatever happens will have to come from the few of us who still have a real stake in the outcome. Let's walk down to Rita's place. Russell's there waitin' for us and as usual he's got a lot to say about things."

As we headed down the hill I said, "Sounds serious."

"Jay, I don't know what it all sounds like. We're hopin' you can help us make sense of the whole thing. You know the situation here as well as we do and you also know what's happenin' on the outside."

Our timing was perfect. Three men were walking out as we reached the café entrance. "Good," Jack said quietly. "It's best that we keep things to just our little group for now."

We all exchanged greetings while Rita set a pot of her strong coffee on the table, then settled into our chairs and filled our cups. Russell looked around the table and asked, "Okay, who's in charge of this little gathering?"

I smiled and spoke up. "Well, since Jack is still the Police Chief that makes him the highest ranking official in Encino so I think he should take the lead."

I'm pretty sure that Jack actually blushed. Since he'd first donned his police uniform and confronted the miners that day at The Bond he'd changed somehow. That morning when I'd watched the TV news coverage of the arrests at the mine and saw him taking charge it was like I was looking at a different person.

"Okay," he said, "We all know a thing or two about what's goin' on so let's share what we know and try to get the big picture. Jay, you probably know all kinds of stuff we don't. You start."

I wasn't sure what my role in this group was supposed to be. I was a writer, a documentarian and I didn't have any physical or financial investment in the town. My investment was strictly emotional. All I could offer were the things I'd read and heard from my sources. "Okay, let me bring you all up to date on what I know about the mine."

They sat attentively while I told them how within days of the documentary being aired there were signs that the story had struck a nerve, a very raw nerve with the executives of American Mining. *The Albuquerque Journal* reported how the documentary had created a major public relations problem for the company. The news about the internal corruption that had closed the mine had rattled the stockholders more than the story of what had happened to Encino. The suggestion that American Mining had deliberately killed the town was playing out all over social media but not in the boardroom. Thousands of people were talking about how the greedy corporate suits had ruined the lives of everyone in the town, and their comments demanded compensation for all of them. It was a huge mess and American was scrambling for a strategy to make it go away.

When I was finished the group sat silently for a moment, looking at each other. Finally Russell spoke up. "Jay, we're all in the same fix here, we can only hang on for so long, but I think we all agree that we can't just sit and watch what American does next. We need to be an equal partner in the process and that means we'll need leverage. They have the deep pockets and all we have are empty buildings. How does that translate to leverage or some kind of power?"

I nodded in agreement. "Your power is in everything around you and the way it looks to the public. Empty streets and buildings, especially empty homes carry a lot of emotional power and I think that's where you start."

"I don't know," Jack said, shaking his head in disagreement, "that tour company looked at our empty little town and didn't see anythin' but amusement and profit."

Russell chimed in, "There's always going to be those assholes who see a way to make money from someone else's misfortune. That's life, but I had a thought and it's sort of what you just said, Jay. If American does intend to open the mine back up they'll need workers and those workers will need a town to live in. If a guy looking for a mining job came here tomorrow he'd take a look at this place and say "No way I'm bringing my family here." I gotta believe that American realizes that."

Rita leaned forward. "Look, I just run a small business here not a big corporation but I know what's going on. You just watch. No matter what we want it will all come down to the money and the stockholders, not us."

I leaned back, coffee in hand, and listened as the opinions circled the table. Emotions were running high and consensus seemed out of reach. After a few minutes I chimed in, "Okay, here's where I think you are. You're in a stand-off with American but they don't know it yet and that's to your advantage. Both sides want the same thing but neither side can do it alone."

Jack let out a long sigh. "American knows exactly what's here and what isn't. They know there's only a handful of us left and I doubt if they're shakin' in their shiny shoes about any kind of resistance. Those guys are experts at playin' hardball."

I looked at Rita and Russell for their reactions and didn't see any sign of disagreement. During my work on the documentary I'd developed a real affection for Encino, just like my father had. And the three people who sat at the table with me were like friends in every sense of the word. There was no question that my documentary had brought attention, both wanted and unwanted, to their dusty little town and I felt some sense of obligation to them. I topped off my coffee, leaned back and asked, "You folks have been playing defense for two years. How do you feel about going on offense?"

There was no reply, just confused expressions. After a moment Russell asked, "What do you mean by offense?"

"Like I told you a minute ago the documentary started a PR nightmare for American, a big black eye. The whole state thinks they're the bad guys and you're the good guys. Let's leverage that. We'll have to let them know that Encino isn't necessarily going to play nice in the sandbox. If they want a working mine they'll have to give you a working town."

Jack was nodding and I could tell he understood. "And by a workin' town you mean fix the place up."

"Yep, and not just a coat of paint and a few windows. We're talking new traffic lights, street signs and a facelift to city hall and the school. We're talking help from the banks to underwrite loans to reopen businesses and buy houses."

"And what if they just tell us "no way"? They have deep pockets and they can just out-wait us until we cave."

"No, there's more to it than that." I answered. "Even without the bad public image to deal with, the company has stockholders who lost money because of the silver theft. They know there's more copper sitting under that ground and they want to cut their losses. The clock is ticking and they want things to happen sooner not later."

Jack was nodding and smiling. "You know, I think I just came up with our first offensive play." He stood up and walked over to the window. "Joe Theobald just pulled up." he said, still smiling. "Keep in mind that the main access road between the mine and the railhead crosses over Joe's land. They've been payin' him a nice fee for the right of way but what would happen if he decided to not renew the deal?"

Russell's eyes widened. "They'd have to cut a new road through the State land at the far western edge of town, in the totally opposite direction from the mine. That'd be another twenty-five miles or more for their trucks to drive every trip to the railhead, each way every day. And the state would make them pay for the road."

I smiled and listened as the ideas ricocheted among them.

By the time Joe had opened the café door the group was buzzing about their plan. Joe joined them at the table and I just sat there listening and taking it all in. The sadness I'd seen in their eyes and heard in their voices had been replaced with a careful optimism and even hope. A strategy was being laid out. Battle lines were being drawn. Part of me was excited by their enthusiasm but another part wondered how these good and simple folks could ever stand up to a confrontation with a huge, influential corporation. I knew that public opinion would only take them so far. And I wondered what these nice people would do if the struggle came right to the streets of Encino. Like it or not I was back in the middle of a story.

Wade Teller
~ Side B

Out of the Blue

When you're checking your email and see a message from a famous person the first thing that pops into your head is "Oh shit, that's fake. I got hacked". That morning when I saw a message from Country music star Wade Teller my fingers instinctively reached for the delete key but something stopped me. I didn't press it. I stared at the name and the tagline that read "I like your work".

A long moment of doubt and a touch of ego led to "What the hell, why not?" and I opened it.

I was surprised that the message had come from Wade himself and not his production company or manager. It was short and to the point. "Jay, I really enjoyed your documentary on Encino, especially the way you handled the feelins' of the people. I have a project idea that I think you'd be perfect for. Please call me at the number below. Thanks. Wade Teller."

The decision to open the message hadn't taken too long but the decision to make the phone call took a lot longer. My writing and producing had been for clients like *PBS* and *The History Channel* along with a handful of universities and corporations. It was a real leap of faith to think a project for a ten-time Grammy winning Country singer could be in the same league. I got up from my desk and made a cup of coffee. It was a total stalling maneuver but it gave me a few minutes to think about things. By the time I'd gotten back across the room and walked a circle around my desk I had caved. Wade freaking Teller wanted to talk to me! I grabbed my phone and punched in the number.

It rang twice then went to his voicemail prompt. I was mentally composing a message to leave when he answered, "Wade here, what's up?"

I took a breath and said, "Wade, hi, this is Jay Rorbach, the documentary writer. I just saw your email message so I'm calling you back."

"Oh yeah, thanks for gettin' back to me, appreciate it. Hey, I really liked that piece you did on Encino,. I watched that thing three times and I wanted to talk to you about maybe workin' on somethin' like that for me. Interested?"

"Well, I don't know. I'm glad you liked the Encino story but I guess I need to know more about what you have in mind before I can say anything more. I'm a historian, first and foremost."

"I get ya' and that's exactly what I need, someone to write my history, my life, and do it up right and truthful."

"Well, that's what I do but I have to wonder about your idea because it seems like there's already been a hell of a lot of stuff written about you. What could I possibly add?"

He let out a boisterous laugh. "You sure got that right. People have written all kinds of stuff about me, some of it true, some not and most of it, well, let's just say it was little too colorful, especially all the gossip and shit from my two ex-wives."

I smiled. "Yeah, that's the stuff I remember." ell, I guess that comes with the territory as they say. A life on the road brings on all kinds of shit but I need somebody, somebody like you, to paint the real picture, like you did for those good folks in Encino. I'm not gettin' any younger and I decided this upcomin' tour will be my last. I'm too old to be sittin' on a bus and partyin' all night so I'm just gonna' do a little studio work from now on. I want the fans to remember all the good stuff."

I couldn't deny that it was a tempting proposition but it was so totally different from any project I'd ever worked on and I wanted to be cautious. My professional reputation was solid. I wondered if delving into the wild and crazy music world could change that. After a few more seconds of thinking it over I decided it was at least worth considering. For the next twenty minutes we talked about his ideas and how we could set up a meeting.

I'd decided to wait until she got home to tell Katie about the call. She was a huge Wade Teller fan and I was almost certain that she'd want to join me when I met with him. That evening when she walked through the door I must have had some kind of odd expression on my face because she looked at me and said, "Uh oh, that's your "guess what happened today" look."

I had already poured the wine. I handed her a glass and said, "Yep, let's go out on the patio. I think you're going to be excited about this."

My butt was no sooner in the chair when she said, "Alright, let's hear it."

Her bemused expression only made me more eager to give her my news. "Well, I got an email this morning which led to a phone conversation which led to a possible television project."

She nodded and waited to see if more explanation was coming, then said. "Okay, that's good news but so far not that exciting."

"The project would be a video biography of Wade Teller, hopefully something we can put on *Country Music Television* or *Entertainment Tonight,* maybe even *American Masters.* He contacted me and we talked on the phone this morning. We're going to meet here in Albuquerque on the fourteenth when his tour brings him to town." I waited a moment for her to respond but her wide eyes and open mouth told me she was too surprised to say much. "And you'll be glad to know that you'll be coming with me for our backstage meeting. I assume you'd like to."

"Holy shit honey, are you serious? I mean, is this a real thing?"

"Yeah, at least the meeting is. He asked me to put together a draft agreement and an outline of how the process will work. If I say yes it will involve going along with him and his band on a few gigs. We'll probably make a trip or two to Nashville and then start interviewing him and a bunch of people. I'll also have to do a ton of research on his history and personal life.

"Wow, that is so cool, a history geek like you working for a music star!"

"Yeah, I agree it's gonna be a stretch. I also asked Saul to join us. Now that he's living here in Albuquerque it'll be easy for him to be part of the decision on whether we want to do it."

"You mean you might say no? Are you crazy?"

"Relax, babe, it's just that it's uncharted territory for me and I want to be sure. A documentary about a superstar singer is not in my comfort zone and I have to admit it's got me a little uneasy. We're probably going to do it but it's going to be a lot different from all my other projects. Wade seems to know exactly what he wants this to be. He and his band are constantly in motion and that means I would be too. Traveling, covering rehearsals, interviewing a ton of people and doing my normal kind of research will make for a pretty crazy schedule. Add Saul's often unpredictable behavior to the mix and it'll probably be one hell of a ride."

Katie was silent for a moment. She took a sip of wine and said, "I guess I hadn't thought about all of that. It sounds like you could be gone a lot which doesn't exactly make me happy but just think of what this opportunity could do for your career. Honey, this is the big time!"

"Yeah, I guess it is but it's nothing even close to what I'm used to doing."

"Honey, you know the old saying, life begins at the end of your comfort zone."

Everything she'd said had already played through my mind a hundred times. The positives and negatives pretty much balanced each other out. "Babe, if you're okay with it I think I'm gonna tell Wade it's a go."

She let out a long sigh. "Go ahead, this is too big to pass up. But remember you're the documentarian and the finished product will have your name on it and your brand. Please, just do what you can to keep Wade from controlling your every move. He's a big star, not someone from a little place like Encino. He's used to getting his way and I'm guessing he'll try calling the shots."

I knew she was right and I knew that would be easier said than done. I nodded and answered, "You got it, babe."

"Welcome to the Music World"

There are a lot of stadiums bigger than University Stadium in Albuquerque but it's still impressive to look out from the upper boxes and see over thirty thousand bodies filling the seats. Over the years Wade's popularity had driven the change from the band performing in small clubs to filling huge arenas and stadiums. Katie, Saul and I were waiting for him to come and lead us down to the stage in the middle of the field. It was nearly an hour before the *Still Wild in the West Tour* concert was scheduled to start but there was already an electric kind of feel in the place.

Saul stood by himself at the railing, studying the scene below. "I'm glad I got those new lenses for the video camera. Stadium crowds are tough to capture in a normal shot." He turned back toward us. "It's not exactly Woodstock down there but that's still a whole hell of a lot of people." His huge smile told me he was already tuned into working on the project.

Katie chimed in, "It's going to be so much easier for you guys to work together now that you've moved here." Saul nodded.

I couldn't resist commenting, "Yeah, at first I told myself that you moved here because of the work but I know it was really because you couldn't find a woman when you were living in little Santa Rosa."

He grinned. "Yep, a small town makes for slim pickings but now, a bigger city and more possibilities. Who knows?"

Katie looked over my shoulder and her expression told me that Wade himself had arrived. I turned just as he reached us and I said, "Hey, Wade, I'm Jay. It's nice to finally meet you."

We shook hands and he said with a big grin, "Same here, Jay. And who are these nice folks?"

Katie didn't wait for me. She stepped forward and offered her hand. "Hi, Wade, I'm Katie Rorbach." She looked star struck.

He took hold of her hand. "Well it's a real pleasure to meet you, Katie." He turned toward Saul. "I'm guessin' you're the camera guy. I liked your work on that Encino show."

Saul was smiling ear to ear. "Thanks, man, Saul Worth. Glad you liked it."

Wade hadn't mentioned the very large and very quiet bald man who'd walked in with him and stood a few feet to his left. Wade saw me staring and said, "Oh, I'm sorry. Everyone, this is Carl, my security chief." We all said hello but Carl just stood there stiffly with a slight nod of his head in our general direction. Even though he wasn't a young man he still looked like he could pick me up and throw me across a room. Something about him made me feel very uncomfortable.

Wade looked out over the stadium with his arms out and a satisfied look on his face. "Look at that crowd, you can feel the energy." He paused then added, "You can feel the love."

I couldn't deny the part about the energy. Tens of thousands of people under a setting sun with the warm-up music playing from the stadium's sound system combined to create a level of excitement that was palpable. Wade turned toward me. "Let's head down to the dressin' room, well it's really the locker room. I don't have much time to talk about your contract but we can at least get things started and y'all can meet the band."

Carl kept himself between us and Wade as we walked. We used a private elevator down to the ground level and when the doors opened the pungent smell of weed greeted us. It came as no surprise. We were standing smack in the middle of The Wade Teller Band and their pre-concert activities. A stadium security guard gave us our media badges and wristbands so we'd be able to access the entire venue. The road crew already had their instruments on stage and were busy working on sound checks, lighting and equipment hook-ups. The JumboTron screens were showing the activity on the stage. Wade introduced us as "the documentary guys" and everyone mingled and shook hands. Super Fan Katie already knew all of their names and I couldn't help but notice Saul's expression as he talked with the keyboard player and backup vocalist, a pretty, young redhead named Lana.

I handed Wade a printed copy of the draft contract. "Look this over when you get some time. It's pretty much my standard production agreement and I listed the specific tasks related to following you guys on your tour. My reimbursable expenses are shown in there too."

Wade flipped through the pages in a ridiculously short time then folded them and stuffed the whole thing into the back pocket of his jeans. "Okay, but I need to talk to you about my ideas first and how I want the thing to look. It's gotta make me look good, you know, to the fans."

It was an odd comment and I answered, "You obviously have a huge fan base and that'll be obvious in the video work we'll do. Every documentary starts out with a basic idea, some kind of angle but I can tell you from experience that things happen along the way. We do research, we find things that add to the story or give it a new slant. We really do our homework to make it the best possible story it can be."

Wade looked puzzled, as though what I'd said was a complete surprise. "What do you mean by all this research and homework you do? What's all that about?"

"Well, a lot of it is historic stuff, like going way back in time. In this case we'd want to learn about your hometown, your childhood, what kind of kid you were. What were your mom and dad like, and your siblings? What about your extended family and how you got started in music? That kind of research."

Wade nodded. "I can give you all that stuff myself. There's a lot of that kind of thing on my website. I have a bunch of boxes of family pictures, all kinds of concert video and even a couple of old home movies so you won't need to do a lot of diggin'."

Katie's warning crossed my mind. I had a growing feeling that he wanted to control the process and that simply wasn't the way things worked. It seemed odd to me and even a little mysterious. I wished that Saul would have been in on the conversation but he was still focused on Lana and out of earshot. In the past my projects had involved working with clients who had a committee or review board that I met with periodically to track my progress. Working on a project that put all of the control into the hands of one man didn't make sense. To me it was a deal breaker and I couldn't leave it out there hanging. I took a breath and said, "Wade, I understand that you want this documentary to be a success and tell your story. When we talked on the phone you said you liked how we worked with the people in Encino. Well, here's the thing. Every one of those folks gave us their trust. We honored that trust and that's why their story resonated so much with the audience. That's what we'll do with you. You'll just have to trust us too."

Wade just looked at me blankly for a moment and then shrugged. "Well, Jay, I hear what you're sayin' about trust and I agree. Let me look over your contract to see what's gonna be happenin' and if I need to make any changes."

I'd known from our first phone call that he'd be a handful as a client so I'd built a big bullshit factor into my fees. I had no clue as to what contract changes he had in mind but my fee wasn't negotiable. He'd named his final tour *"Still Wild in the West"* and if I was going to be a part of it I was going to be compensated accordingly. Nobody was going to get wild with my money.

We got to watch the concert from a private box that Wade had arranged for us. It wasn't the same experience as the ground level seats provided but it gave us the chance to hear each other over the music as we planned what to do when it came time for us to go to work on the project. Katie wanted to be part of things and we'd worked out a way for her to do face-to-face interviews with the band members and the fans. Saul would help her with video in addition to the large scale taping of the event. I was already outlining the story structure. The project was starting to feel real and I was still nervous about it.

Hitting the Road

After only two days to make the arrangements we were ready to follow the tour. Looking at it as a little adventure, Katie had taken a few days of personal time away from the office. Her hair pulled back and braided into a ponytail and her bandana scarf reminded me of how she looked when we had first met in college. Saul had trimmed his beard but still wore the look of a Bohemian artist. I thought that my jeans and black polo shirt were the right combination of professional and partier. Saul had organized a large array of camera and sound equipment and I'd rented us a van. A sizeable good faith advance check from Wade had allayed most of my concerns about the way things might go. We headed across I-40 through some of the most beautiful high desert scenery in the country and on to Phoenix for the next concert stop. I had only a vague idea of what to expect.

One crowded van, three excited people and seven long hours made for quite a journey. We weren't college kids on an adventure like we'd once been and when we reached the crest of a hill on I-17 the Phoenix skyline was a welcome sight. We had made reservations at the Westin, the same hotel as the band and we checked in just before their bus arrived. It was almost an hour later when Saul knocked on our door and suggested we all go down to the lobby bar. We had a very loose list of things we wanted to do before we left for Chase Field and the concert. The one definite item was meeting with Wade and getting a signed contract. My version of a contract.

The lobby of the Westin was spacious and colorful. It had the look of a place where a party might break out at any moment. The bartender had just set a cold beer in front of me when Wade rushed in with Carl close behind. "Alright, Jay, we gotta talk fast, the van's sittin' out there waitin' for us." He laid the contract on the bar in front of me and dropped on to the barstool next to mine.

In the past I'd had the luxury of time to negotiate my agreements with clients but it was obvious that wouldn't be happening with Wade. It was looking like every detail of the project would be done on the fly. "I'll need some time to give it a final look-over," I said, as I picked it up, "especially since we've already gotten started."

"I get it, I know you probably think things are movin' too fast but that's just the way my business is. You can't let any grass grow under your feet." I could tell from his grin that doing business at hyper-speed was totally normal to him. He looked down at the bar and muttered, "Bernie Sheltin from Limelight Partners, he's my business manager, the guy that handles this sorta thing. I learned a long time ago that I'm no business man. Anyway, he said I shouldn't sign it yet. He wants to put in some language about who you should interview and that kind of thing. He glanced at Carl and added, "He's still kinda' nervous about the research stuff you wanna' do." I saw Carl nodding in agreement.

I wanted to say something like, "Would you please just knock it off with the research shit?" but I settled for, "Wade, I promise you it'll be fine and you'll get to see everything we come up with in advance and then approve it or not."

He nodded and let out a deep sigh. "Okay, I'll call off Bernie." He grabbed a pen that was clipped to my credit card receipt on the bar and signed the contract. We shook on it and he said, "Okay then, "let's get this story started." Before I could say anything more he was headed for the band at the front door. Katie had been sitting on the other side of me and when Wade and Carl were out of earshot she leaned over and asked, "What in the hell is his problem with who you talk to?"

I didn't have a clear answer for her and just said, "I don't know but I have a feeling it's just a matter of time before we find out."

It was a twenty minute van ride to the stadium and the band was already revved up for the show, A woman was working her way down the aisle putting official security wristbands on everyone. Saul had somehow managed to land the seat beside Lana and their conversation was non-stop and full of smiles. When we reached the stadium and got out of the van we knew the clock was ticking. We had a lot to do before the band got on stage and the lights went up. Katie carried a microphone and recorder while Saul followed her with a hand-held video camera.

The crowd noise was already overwhelming and any conversations were shouted not spoken. The two of them interviewed fans as they filed into the stadium while I meandered through the crowd shouting my observations into my own recorder. Just before the show started Saul went back to the van and switched cameras then worked his way up to the stadium box level to get a view of the entire event.

There was a lot to take in and not much time to do it. When a security guard motioned to me that the gates would be closing I found Katie and we hurried inside with the last throng of fans. For the next two hours while over forty thousand fans swayed and cheered and enjoyed themselves the three of us continued working on a kind of documentary that was a total departure from our previous projects. The volume of the music, the ground-level energy and the party-like atmosphere were almost intoxicating. I thought to myself, "Man, a guy could get used to this kind of work."

For the first half hour Saul carried his new wide angle camera and moved along the railings of the upper deck, shooting the concert from above and panning the huge crowd. It took him another half hour to work his way back down to the field and set up in front of the stage. Katie and I stood off to one side near the stage and caught an amusing glimpse of our videographer friend moving with the music while somehow managing to keep his camera rock-steady.

We had arranged with the band that when they began their final set we'd start making our way back up to a private box for an after-concert party. When we heard the first chords of their signature song, *What's Left of my Heart,* the three of us headed for the elevator. Katie commented that it was the first time in her life she'd felt like a VIP. A few minutes later the elevator doors opened and we were instantly in the middle of a party that was already well underway.

When Wade, the band and of course Carl finally came through the door things got louder and wilder. It took us awhile to find our way through the crowded room to the spot by the bar where Wade was holding court. Despite being in his late sixties with some wrinkles and gray hair he'd kept himself in great shape and had the look of a handsome, rugged cowboy. He'd always had a large number of female fans and like it or not our attempts at a conversation with him had to be shared with a variety of smiling, starry eyed women of all ages.

Through the steady din of voices and crowd noise I told him that I'd signed our contract and that we were ready to kick the project into high gear. He smiled, leaned close and shouted into my ear, "That's great, man, I'll give it to Bernie. He was askin' about it. This is goin' to be fun!" The word "fun" hadn't been a part of the work I'd done in the past but I'd already learned that Wade Teller saw the world from a whole different angle than I did.

It was a cloudy morning and we stashed our equipment and climbed back into our van around noon. It was getting dark by the time we got back to Albuquerque. The drive back from Phoenix had been different than the drive getting there, probably due to the larger amount of alcohol and fewer hours of sleep than we were all used to the night before. We joked about getting too old to be groupies and it was easy to fall asleep that night despite a head full of thoughts.

By the time I'd drained my third cup of morning coffee it was easier to focus on what I'd be doing for the next few months. I had a contract, an outline for the script and a good start on the photos and video footage. There would be more face-time with Wade in the near future but our main task at this point was getting to Nashville, his birthplace and still his hometown. Saul and I would tape interviews with the people on Wade's list and then Saul would go out on his own to capture images of Wade's past like his old house, school and neighborhood. I'd move on to do what I was used to doing on my projects; historical research. It was the core of the project and the part that Wade was mysteriously nervous about. My gut told me there'd be surprises ahead.

Looking for the Story

As soon as we'd landed in Nashville I called Katie. She was back to her routine at the hospital and she'd been enjoying telling her friends about her concert adventure and meeting Wade Teller the superstar. If everything went well with the interviews and our research I'd be back home in three days. Given the two hour time difference and a delay with our flight we got to our hotel just in time for happy hour. Somehow leaning back and downing a little alcohol seemed like a fitting way to start this new project.

Saul was sitting beside me at the bar and was more focused on his cellphone than the glass of Scotch in front of him. I was close enough to see the screen and the name "Lana Stafford". I leaned toward him, grinning. "Well, is your time with Lana going to be personal or can we bill Wade for it?" I never saw anyone switch off a phone so quickly.

Look," he said sheepishly, "I just figured why not make the most of the situation. I have to be here in Nashville to work on the project and she'll be back here tomorrow after the tour is over. There's no harm in spending a little time with her, is there?"

"Not at all, in fact I'd be surprised if you didn't."

"I figure we can get the interviews done tomorrow and I'll still have a couple of days to do the still shots and video. I assume you'll still be holed up at the courthouse or the newspaper."

"Yeah, I'll do my digging in the archives and then head back here. The hotel bar is nice and I can do my narrative write-up from there. I assume your evening activity will happen elsewhere."

"Yeah, hopefully at her place."

I couldn't resist. "See, moving out of Santa Rosa is already paying off."

Our workday started early. Wade had contacted a few people to let them know we'd be getting in touch and I had a short list of names and phone numbers that he'd compiled. He asked me to please stick with just the names on the list which only increased my concerns about his intent. The names included his younger sister, a boyhood friend, a minister, a high school teacher, a former member of the band, a bartender at a club where he'd performed and, strangely, a retired Nashville cop. Those folks would probably provide some interesting background if I asked the right questions, my questions not Wade's. That would give me the human side of the story. My time digging into files at a newspaper or courthouse usually gave me the facts and details that formed the historical framework for a documentary but I already had a feeling this time would somehow be different.

Nashville was everything I'd expected and more. I had a lot to accomplish while I was there but on a short walk around town the distractions came at me non-stop. Things like standing on the sidewalk gawking at the Ryman Auditorium and feeling like a tourist. That feeling grew larger when I saw The Grand Ole Opry. It was impossible to look at it and keep all of those great classic Country songs from playing in my head. I promised myself right then and there that I'd be coming back with Katie.

It was a hectic morning contacting the people on the list but we managed to talk with all of them, some on the phone and some in person. Saul got some good video of the on-site, face to face interviews. It was obvious why Wade had selected those folks because every one of them gushed over what a wonderful and talented person he was. I even suspected that he had given them their little scripts to rehearse. It didn't feel like it did back when I was getting the honest emotions of the folks in Encino.

Because it was closer to our hotel, after the interviews I went to the newspaper's office first. *The Tennessean* was a typical big-city paper but it was particularly known for its archives on the history and people of Country music. After a twenty minute wait the Archives Manager led me down a long corridor to a large room with rows and rows of old file cabinets and metal shelving. I set my laptop case down on a table next to a large microfiche reader. "I apologize," she said with a smile, "We're still working on transferring all the back issues from fiche to computer and I'm afraid this is where you're going to have to do your research."

"Oh, that's okay, I've done a whole lot of my work on these old machines."

She nodded and asked, "So how can I help you get started? What or who are you looking for here?"

"I'm looking for some background on Wade Teller and his family."

The woman was silent for a moment and I couldn't quite read her expression. I waited and she finally said, "Hmm, the man comes from quite a family, any particular person or relative you're focused on?" It seemed like an odd question.

"No, just the family in general, his parents and siblings, grandparents, you know, his roots, what kind of people he came from."

She had an odd smile. "Well, all I can say is you've got your work cut out for you with all that." Before she walked away she said, "That yellow card on the table will tell you what to do if you want to print things and what it will cost. There's a coffee machine through that door and if you need me for anything just head back down the hallway." There was a pause and then, "Good luck."

I opened up my laptop and took out the list of names, dates and places that Wade had put together for me so I could see what was still left to do. For the first half hour I jotted down notes on the few articles and photos I'd found that related to the Teller family and Googled a few things that led to links. It was pretty boring stuff, mostly weddings and funerals but when I Googled a couple of names from those photos things got a lot more interesting. The names weren't on Wade's list. Earl Rollins was Wade's maternal grandfather and David "Sonny" Walsh was Wade's uncle. Those guys didn't just show up in wedding photos, they also appeared in articles and photos where they were being led to jail by Nashville and Tennessee state police. I leaned back in my chair and stared at the screen. I was struck by how much Wade resembled his grandfather, the grandfather who'd been charged with robbery and moving stolen merchandise. I flipped to the photo of Sonny, the uncle who'd been arrested for receiving stolen merchandise and assault. My thoughts of scandal were interrupted when my cellphone vibrated. It was Saul.

"Hey, man," I answered. "How are the photos going?"

"So far so good. I got stills of his family home and his school, the church he went to and some video of his old neighborhood. It's pretty boring stuff to be honest. How's your research moving along? I hope it's more interesting than what I've been doing."

Since I wasn't sure what, if anything the newspaper photos meant I decided to not mention them. "Oh, it's pretty boring here too. I'm going to give it another couple of hours and then try to get over to the courthouse which will probably be even more boring than this."

"I've got a couple more shots to take from Wade's list and then I'll be running out of good daylight. I'll meet you back at the hotel bar around six or six-thirty."

"That works for me, see you then."

It felt too soon to say anything to Saul about Wade's relatives. There seemed to be some bad apples on the family tree but a lot of families could say that. Until I dug into the stories enough to know some details I couldn't be sure if they had any connection to Wade.

"Give the guy the benefit of the doubt" I thought, but even if there was no connection I couldn't resist getting back to those newspaper articles. I'd read a story about how Grampa Earl was part of a statewide ring of thieves who specialized in stealing and fencing furs, guns and jewelry. It seemed like your run of the mill kind of crime until I read that the ring was believed to be a part of the Dixie Mafia. I knew about the mafia in Italy and New York and Chicago and even Las Vegas but the Dixie Mafia was a new one to me. Once again Google had brought me surprises. The Dixie Mafia first appeared in Biloxi, Mississippi in the 1960s and it was still in operation. It was involved in just about any type of crime a person could think of. There were numerous references to its ties to the Chicago mob and that the group was active throughout the southeast United States.

I'd often felt that I'd spent way too much of my life buried up to my neck in history. In the course of doing research for my documentaries I'd learned all kinds of obscure facts and bits of information that I'd never found a use for later on. And now I'd learned a new one, that there was a sort of hillbilly crime machine operating throughout the South. Like with most people my exposure to mob crime had come from movies and television, men in expensive suits driving nice cars, not men in jeans and flannel shirts driving pickups. While the Dixie Mafia had operated regularly in Southern cities like Nashville it was also active in rural areas.

I sat there staring at the screen, at an article about a truckload of stolen merchandise impounded by police with a photo of three men standing in handcuffs beside the truck. One of them was Earl Rollins, good old Grampa Earl from Wade's wedding photos. I looked closer at the line of young Tennessee state troopers standing behind them and recognized one of them. The big, burly one on the right was Carl, Wade's security chief.

Suddenly Wade's insistence on controlling my research was becoming more clear.

From our very first phone conversation, when he'd told me how some of the things that had been written about him were "a little too colorful" I'd been expecting something like that photo to pop up sooner or later. Only instead of colorful I'd call it scandalous or criminal. A feeling inside me knew the photo meant something big so I sent it to a scanner and printer. It definitely seemed like something I should have in my files.

Allowing a few hours for the newspaper research had seemed like enough when I'd first calculated my fees but after just an hour and a half I knew it wasn't. Finding a bunch of old publicity photos from Wade's early days of performing was the low hanging fruit of my work. Crime photos were a totally different thing. A few branches of Wade's family tree seemed like they could take my research in a whole other direction and consume a lot more time. The easy route would be to ignore that part of his story and just stick to the music. Experience had taught me that taking the easy route usually resulted in getting only half the story. That just wasn't my style.

Local Color

It was an enjoyable walk back to the hotel. After a little dive into the minibar in my room and a nice, long phone conversation with Katie I headed down to the lobby. I wasn't surprised that Saul was already settled on a stool but I hadn't expected to see the lovely redheaded keyboardist sitting next to him. "Well, looks like we'll have a local girl joining us tonight," I said as I reached the bar.

Saul smiled. "Yeah, well I just thought Lana could help us fill in a few blanks about Wade's life here in Nashville." It was an attempt at an explanation but based on his expression and how beautiful she looked I didn't buy it for a second.

I shook hands with Lana. "Nice to see you again," I said, hoping I didn't appear to be intruding on their date.

"Hi, Jay, it's nice to see you too. Saul said it'd be okay to join you guys for a drink."

"It's more than okay. In fact when Saul said you'd be back in town today I wondered how we might talk you into meeting us for a little while." I could tell from Saul's expression that he didn't like the "meeting us" part when he had thought of it as "meeting him". I added, "But I'm sure you two already have plans."

There was enough awkwardness to go around. I was glad when Lana said, "Well, I've got time on my hands now that I won't be tourin' anymore and I wanted to show Saul some of the places I like to go when I'm in town. Since they're some of the same places where Wade performed I thought you might enjoy seein' them too."

Saul chimed in, "Yeah, but just for a while, in case Lana and I might want to take off by ourselves."

There it was, the evening plans were clear and I knew exactly how I fit into them. "Got it. Lana, just lead the way." I took Saul aside and talked him into running up to his room and grabbing his handheld video camera so we could get a taste of the street life at night.

It was a long walk or a short Uber ride to the Honky Tonk Highway area but since it was a warm evening we opted for the walk. Lana was a treasure trove of local history and as we walked she let me record her. This stretch of city streets was an eclectic mix of businesses including some of the old bars and juke joints that had given a start to a lot of Country singers. It was a 365 day a year tourist attraction but still a place for the local music crowd to gather.

We made a quick stop at a bar called Springwater so Lana could introduce us to their house specialty, Fruit Tea. It was a sweet whiskey drink that she said the locals referred to as "a headache in a glass". I ordered a beer. She took us to Jason Aldean's Rooftop Bar and we watched the raucous mix of music fans and drinkers. About half an hour later she stood up and announced, "Okay, it's time to move on. You gotta see Tootsie's Orchid Lounge next. All kinds of folks have played there like Willie Nelson and Patsy Cline and of course, Wade." She seemed to be getting into the spirit of our project and I welcomed it.

As soon as we walked through Tootsie's front door I was mesmerized. Lana could read my face and shouted over the crowd noise, "You could make a documentary about this place all by itself!"

She was right. The long bar, the colorful neon signs, the stage lighting and the Wall of Fame with photographs of the Country music royalty who had performed there over the years were more than a person could take in on one visit. I was staring at the photos when a man's voice behind me called out, "Lana, you're back!" I turned to see a skinny, bearded man hugging her.

"Hi, Ben! Yeah, we finished in Vegas, no more tourin' all over the country. Wade stayed back to meet some folks to go over the engineerin' for the new album. He'll be back next week. I decided to head straight for home. Guys, this is Ben Strong. He's one of the managers here."

We all shook hands and exchanged names. Lana leaned in and said, "Ben, I don't know if you heard but these guys are makin' a documentary about Wade. They're here in town to get some background stuff on his life, you know, local color."

Ben grinned. "Well, guys, Wade's a hometown boy and there's lots of folks around here who can tell you some stories. Of course some of the stories might be a little on the risqué side. He cut a pretty wide path in his younger days and he comes from a wild and wooly kinda family." The words were no sooner out of his mouth when I saw Lana's raised eyebrows. He cleared his throat, turned and pointed toward the stage. "Uh, and we like to think that's the place where he really got his start."

There it was again, a reference to his family but it didn't seem like the time or place to dig into that. Saul interrupted, "Ben, would it be okay if I got some video of the place?

"Oh hell yeah, we're used to cameras around here. The tourists love to take pictures and the staff doesn't even notice it anymore."

Lana put her arm around Saul's waist and said, "I'll kind of guide him around the place if you guys want to talk some more." Saul winked at me and off they went.

Suddenly and a bit uncomfortably it seemed like the right time to ask Ben about his comment. "Uh, I'm curious about something you said about Wade's family, about them being wild and wooly. What did you mean by that?"

He hesitated and I could tell he was reluctant to answer me. He had the same expression as the woman at the newspaper archive. He shook his head and said, "Oh that. I didn't mean to give you the wrong impression. All I meant was that Wade comes from a big family and some of his relatives, well they sort of had reputations for...I'm not sure how to say it. They got themselves into some trouble. Let's just let it go at that." He seemed nervous and quickly took a different angle. "Hey, see that guitar hangin' on the wall? That was Wade's first one, the one he learned to play on. He got it from his grandfather."

I thought about it for few seconds then went ahead and asked, "You mean his Grampa Earl?"

I sensed more nervousness. "Oh, so you know that Earl was his grandfather. Did Wade tell you that?"

"No, I was doing some research and I came across his name."

Ben nodded and looked even more uncomfortable. "You know, man, the only thing people need to know about old Earl is that he was the one who helped Wade the most, especially after Wade's Dad died. He bought him that guitar and lessons to go with it. He twisted a few arms to get some bar owners to let him perform on the weekends. Hell, Wade was still in high school but Earl took those owners aside and told them to say Wade was eighteen so he could play in the bars legally. He even bought Wade some fancy Western outfits to wear. Later on he found him a guy, Bernie, to manage all the money that was coming in. Without Earl and Wade's uncle Sonny I don't think Wade would have ever made it big like he did."

Ben's information would be a great addition to the Wade Teller storyline. Family ties were always appealing to viewers. Wade's All American good looks and his media-created image made everyone want to be part of his family. I had no idea if his fans knew much if anything about Grampa Earl. His last name was different from Wade's and they had lived in different cities. Outside of some local folks in Nashville music circles there didn't seem to be a clear connection between the two men. But Wade's instruction that I only interview or research the people on his list still stuck in my head and it only reinforced the conclusion I'd reached earlier: Wade Teller was connected at least in a familial way to someone with a criminal history. Given Grampa Earl's hands-on help to give Wade a start to his career meant to me that any effort to ignore either side of the story would be impossible and even unethical. It was a dilemma I'd never faced before.

Ben still looked uneasy so I wasn't surprised when he told me he had to get back to work. I thanked him and watched him walk behind the bar and talk with a well dressed man who couldn't take his eyes off me as they talked. It was pretty clear that I was the topic of conversation. The man looked all business with no hint of a smile as he nodded and listened to Ben. His scowl was focused on me and I had the distinct feeling my probing questions about Grampa had caused a stir. The man reached into his pocket and pulled out his phone. He punched in a number and began talking. His eyes were back on me. I pretended not to notice but I couldn't deny I was getting nervous. My conversation with Ben had taken an abrupt turn when I mentioned Grampa Earl and it was clear he didn't want to say anything further on the subject. I'd hit a brick wall.

Saul and Lana were walking toward me arm in arm and it was another signal that my work there was over. It was time to leave Tootsie's.

Lana smiled. "Did you and Ben have a good talk?"

"Yeah, I guess. He told me a little bit about Wade and his performing here. I was hoping to hear more but he had to get back to work."

She nodded. "Well, Wade said he'd fill you in on things later so you can get the rest of the story from him when he's back here next week."

Saul handed me his camera. "Hey, man, we're going back to Lana's place, how about getting this back to the hotel for me."

My friend's plans had taken a surprising turn and I was glad for him. "No problem. Let's regroup in the morning and see where we stand with things."

Saul nodded. Lana smiled and said, "Thanks. G'night, Jay."

I took an Uber back to the hotel, stashed my stuff and went down to the lobby bar. My phone conversation with Katie was two bourbons long and I didn't let on that my research had been anything but routine. Saul and I had agreed to book an early afternoon flight back to Albuquerque and I was eager to get home. The phone call and the bourbon ended at the same time and as I waited for the elevator I got a text from Saul. All it said was "I'll be back to the hotel in the morning, talk to you then." My friend seemed to have found a romance or something close to it.

Sleep was hard to come by and my morning coffee in the café helped me focus on my notes. When my phone buzzed I assumed it was Saul but the screen readout was a phone number with a 615 area code. It was from Nashville. When I answered a man's voice asked, "Is this Rorbach?"

"Yes it is, who's this?"

After a pause he said, "This is Carl, Wade's Chief of Security."

I couldn't decide which was more unsettling, the coldness of his voice or the fact that he was calling me directly. I cleared my throat and replied, "Yes, Carl, what can I do for you?"

"Well, for starters I want you to stop askin' so many questions about Wade's family. He gave you a list of people to talk to so stick to them and nobody else. You have no idea what you're messin' with here."

I had a hunch that Carl had been the man on the other end of last night's call to the well dressed man at Tootsie's. The newspaper photo of Grampa Earl in handcuffs and the young Carl standing behind him in his police uniform flashed through my head. At first that photo had seemed like a strange coincidence but now it suddenly seemed like a lot more. Clearly over the years the two men had made some kind of connection. For a moment I couldn't decide if I should be nervous that a very large and intimidating man was checking up on my activities or be pissed off that he was sticking his nose some place it didn't belong. Pissed off won.

"Look, Carl, I'm working for Wade on this project, not you.

"Nope, you're wrong. When you work for Wade you work for me and for Bernie too."

"Nope, *you're* wrong. I work with the man whose name is on the contract and that's Wade and Wade only. If I need anything from you guys I'll ask for it so back off."

For a moment there was silence on the other end of the call, a deep sigh and then, "Look, punk, I'm not goin' to chew on this anymore. Stick to Wade and music and stop askin' so many god damned questions about anythin' or anyone else. You heard what I said so consider yourself warned." He hung up and I sat there for a moment unsure of what had just happened. A call from Saul brought me back to the moment.

"Hey, man, I'm gonna hang out here with Lana awhile longer. I got all of my taping done so how about I meet you in the lobby at eleven?"

"What about your equipment, your bags, all of that?"

"No problem. I'll shower here and she even bought me a toothbrush. All I'll have to do at the hotel is run up to my room and grab my stuff. Sound good?"

There wasn't much I could say. I took a sip of my coffee and said, "Our plane leaves at 1:30 and it'll be traffic the whole way to the airport. Don't be late. I really want to get back home."

Saul must have heard something in my voice and asked, "Everything okay, man?"

"Yeah, I guess so. I have to run back over to the newspaper and check one last thing so I'll be waiting for you in the lobby. I'll call for the Uber ahead of time."

More than it Appears

There was a different woman working in the newspaper archive department and she led me back to the microfiche room where I'd found the photos of Grampa Earl and Uncle Sonny. That first visit revealed the beginnings of the story but I'd uncovered other parts to it. There was the part about Grampa and the Dixie Mafia but now there was a twist, actually several twists. There was the story of how one of the arresting officers that day had become connected to the culprit's family which was also my client's family. And then there was the story of how Bernie Sheltin's firm began managing Wade's career at precisely the same time good ole Grampa was steering things.

Fortunately the woman didn't ask me what I was looking for. I came across a few articles on Wade's local appearances and an advertisement for a local bar with Wade as the headliner. In the photo he looked like a wide eyed kid. I dug through the editions that followed the story of Grampa's arrest and found references to the crimes committed, the testimony of witnesses and the sentences given out. It was a long and winding trail that led to the conclusion that Grampa Earl and Uncle Sonny were liars, thieves and conmen. Their ties to organized crime were real and obvious. And I found another small but interesting side story about one of the Nashville cops who'd been there for the initial arrest. During the trial one Patrolman Carl W. Gibbens had trouble remembering anything meaningful that had happened. He couldn't recall details of the events. He couldn't give direct answers to the prosecution's questions. All in all he came across as totally clueless. The reporter who'd covered the trials wrote how the cop's testimony had badly weakened the case against Grampa, Sonny and the mob.

A half hour of research had provided me with copies of articles and photos that could only be described as a black eye for Wade Teller's good guy image. His big start in the music business had come from the money and influence of criminals. The fact they were his grandfather and uncle didn't make that any less troubling. It was no wonder that he'd wanted me to stick solely to his list of contacts. I knew I'd have to dig further into that part of Wade's life.

There was one last thing I wanted to check out before I packed up my notes; Bernie Sheltin's company, Limelight Partners was part of the story. After a few minutes of online searches of business and entertainment sites I'd turned up almost nothing. Then I found their website and it was the weakest one I'd ever seen, just one page with a picture of an office building in Nashville and Bernie's headshot with the caption *Senior Partner*. Strangely, there were no others partners listed. There was no mention of Wade or any other entertainer they represented, just a lot of fluff about Limelight's services and years in business. I thought to myself that any firm in the entertainment and promotion business would be bragging about the star power of their clients. Their website was far from glamorous and it had an artificial feel to it. There was a phone number listed with the note "Messages Only" and an email address. It made me wonder if there was even a live human being working in their office. Viewing the site only added to the growing number of questions I had about Wade's career.

Saul managed to get back to the hotel on time and we made it to the airport with a little time to spare. We had time for a sandwich and comparing our notes on what we'd accomplished. In terms of the goals we'd set before our trip we were in great shape. We still had to do the one-on-one interview with Wade at his home but the notes, interviews, photos and video we'd done seemed complete at least as far as my original plans were concerned. Coupled with all of the photos and videos Wade had given us we had a huge writing and editing task ahead of us. But I couldn't seem to shake the darker part about Wade's family history. I had some serious decisions to make and it had to be soon.

Sitting at the gate waiting for our flight was the same mind-numbing situation that's a regular part of air travel. Saul passed the time texting with Lana and playing online puzzles. The fact he didn't want to talk about the project was fine with me. Normally this was the point in our collaborations when we'd go down our checklist of tasks and plan out our work for the upcoming weeks but the events of the past twenty four hours called for some quiet time. Saul was clearly smitten with Lana and I was sure he wasn't happy about leaving her behind. I was lost in thought about what I'd stumbled into with my research about Wade's family, his career and his manager. All I knew was that I'd have to talk to Saul first thing in the morning before I spent any more time on the project.

Our flight was uneventful and Katie picked us up at the curb outside the baggage claim. Our Nashville nightlife dominated the conversation in the car and I breathed a sigh of relief when Saul got into his car at my house and headed home. I was in the bedroom changing my clothes and as usual Katie had been reading my face. "You look kind of distant. Are you tired from the trip or is there a problem?"

"Oh, I guess a little of both."

"I get why you'd be tired but what's your problem?"

"I'm not exactly sure. How about you help me figure out some things over a glass of wine."

A few minutes later we were on the patio and I thought about while I'd been gone how much I'd missed our view of the Sangre de Cristos. My work always had me thinking of other places and other people but looking at my wife and those beautiful mountains made me feel rooted and happy. Katie patiently waited for me to start talking and I knew I owed her a briefing on everything that I'd been doing for the past few days. I raised my wine glass and she leaned toward me and clinked hers to mine. I smiled and said, "Here's to being home."

"So fill me in on everything. You didn't say much about the project on our phone calls. Was it a productive trip?"

I nodded. "Yeah, we got pretty much everything on our list. Saul got some great stills and more than enough video. The interviews with the locals were actually kind of fun. Thanks to Saul's new, uh, friendship with Lana we got some local footage that we hadn't even thought of, some good on-the-street kind of stuff."

Katie smirked. "From what you told me on the phone it sounds like more of a romance than a friendship."

"I have to agree. When there's a sleepover involved it's gotta be romantic. He kept asking me if I was sure that I wouldn't need his help when I went back to Nashville to interview Wade."

"Well, I guess I was wondering the same thing. This project hasn't exactly been like your other ones."

I took a long sip and leaned back in my chair. "I think what it comes down to is I have enough information to do the documentary Wade's way but not my way."

"What do you mean by that?"

I wondered how I could explain it to her when I couldn't even explain it to myself. I chose my words carefully. "It's like I told you when I first signed on with Wade. He's got this idea of the documentary being some kind of testament to his fame and success with nothing but sunshine and happy thoughts. He sees it as a Hollywood kind of production and I see it as more like history, the true facts, a documentary which is what I make. And it's what he said he wanted."

"So you're saying that Wade doesn't want the truth."

"He wants *his* version of the truth, the story of a bright-eyed little boy with a dream who grows up to be a big Country star. Unfortunately life isn't always that simple and in his case it's not even close. He wants the documentary to be like the Side A of a record; the hit song, the one all the fans want to hear. But it turns out there's a real Side B to his story, the side no one pays much attention to."

"Uh oh, it sounds like you found out something."

"Yeah, really something! It turns out that Wade Teller didn't get famous on just his talent and charm. He had a grandfather that did all kinds of things to get Wade noticed."

"That sounds kind of sweet, a grandfather helping his grandson get a leg up on his dream."

After another long sip and a deep breath I said, "Honey, the doting grandfather was a gangster, a hillbilly version of one but still a bad guy."

It took Katie a moment before she responded. "What the hell? What do you mean by a gangster? You mean like the mob?

"It's like every project I work on, I'll be looking for one thing and five other things pop up. In this case one of those things was something called the Dixie Mafia."

"Dixie Mafia, is that a real thing?"

"It's real, very real, and it seems that Wade's old Grampa Earl and his Uncle Sonny were full-fledged members of the group. It started out in Biloxi, Mississippi a long time ago and now they're all over the South including Nashville."

"So what does that have to do with Wade?"

"Well, I found out that Grampa bought Wade his first guitar and clothes to wear on stage. Then he pressured different club owners to let Wade perform even before he was legal age. Later on Grampa put the strong arm on a record producer to get Wade into the studio, kind of a test recording with a full back-up band, and then he put some not so friendly pressure on a few radio stations to put it on the air. Those things are borderline illegal and they cost a lot of money. From there it was Wade's talent that got things going but he also had Uncle Sonny calling the shots on the side and keeping a constant eye on things to make sure nobody got in the way.'

Katie leaned back, shaking her head. Finally she said, "I guess that explains why Wade gave you the list of people to talk to. What are you going to do now?"

I'd been dreading the thought of telling her the whole story but I knew it had to come out. "I'm not sure but I guess it will start with a long heart-to-heart with Wade. He told me in our first conversation that he wanted a truthful story but all the people on his list gave us was sugar coating. So I did some digging and I talked to a couple of people who weren't on the list and wow, what a difference!"

Katie was hanging on every word so I kept talking. "It seems that good old Grampa did a little time in jail in between helping Wade. So did Uncle Sonny. Reading through the old news stories and reconstructing the timeline of events it was clear that the money they were using to help Wade had to have come from their criminal activities. Apparently neither of them had a steady job."

"That's going to be a tough conversation with Wade. Are you nervous?"

"Well, there's more. One of the other things I got from the research is that big, unfriendly Carl went from being a Nashville cop to security muscle for Grampa and Sonny, and now Wade." I waited a moment for her reaction before I told her the hard part. "When I was at the hotel waiting for Saul I got a phone call from Carl and he warned me to stop asking questions and talking to the wrong people."

The color drained from her face. "Oh my God, what did you get yourself into here?"

I leaned toward her and held her hands in mine. "Don't worry, babe, no project is worth risking this kind of trouble over. I'm going to talk with Wade, with no Carl around, and tell him everything that's going on. He could very well tell me to stop working and we'll go our separate ways. At least that's what I'm guessing. There's a chance of that."

"What does Saul say about all of this?"

"I haven't told him about it yet. You know how easily he gets rattled and I wanted to think about things for a while and hear your thoughts too. I'll have a long talk with him tomorrow when we meet to look at the tape."

She stared at me with tears in her eyes, shaking her head. "When you first told me about the project I was so excited. It was big time show business stuff and now it's turned into something else, something scary."

I squeezed her hands and said, "Believe me, babe, I'll do the right thing."

The Big Reveal

"You told me we'd be working with musicians. Musicians play guitars and sing, they don't move stolen merchandise. They don't rob people. They don't beat people up."

I was just as upset and frustrated with our situation but it wasn't quite as simple as Saul described it. We'd been trying hard to develop the storyline and images for a documentary and trying just as hard to keep our focus strictly on Wade's career in Country music. He'd made it clear he was ready to retire from touring and described the documentary as his legacy project. Now, just a few weeks into the work my research had turned up a whole lot more than music.

"Hey, man, this is a total surprise to me too. This was supposed to be a straight up story about the life and career of a Country star, nothing more. Obviously there's more here than Wade told us."

"Yeah a whole lot more." Saul was clearly rattled and paced around my office as he talked. "Look, Jay, it's been a fun couple of weeks hanging with Wade and the band and hearing all of their stories. And you know I've developed a pretty strong attachment to Lana. But Wade gave us all that stuff and I got some great stills and hours and hours of video. You can take care of the one on one interview video with Wade so I'm not sure what's left for me to do here besides the editing."

I leaned back in my chair. "It sounds like you want to quit."

Saul stopped pacing and stood there looking out the window. He took a deep breath and turned back toward me. "Truth be told I was hoping for another chance to get back to Nashville. But look, Jay, you know from when we were working in Encino that I get spooked when there's any kind of trouble, anything illegal involved. That's just not the kind of stuff I want anything to do with."

I smiled. "You mean like the little plastic bag of blunts you've been carrying in your shirt pocket for as long as I've known you, that kind of illegal?"

He smirked and nodded. "Okay, so I was a hypocrite then but now it's finally legal. But we're not talking pot here, we're talking about major felonies and it sounds like our client is tied into them somehow, at least indirectly."

I knew Saul was right and I had no plan yet for dealing with the problem. I'd never even heard of the Dixie Mafia until I started to dig into Wade's past. At first glance the Teller family had looked like average folks; a middle class bunch from Nashville who went to church, paid their taxes and never got into anything close to trouble. But like with all my other documentaries I'd done a deep dive into the history of my subject. My deep dives usually turned up a surprise or two but nothing on the level of this one. I knew I had to reassure my nervous friend. "Look, I left Wade a voice message and told him we have to meet to do the one-on-one stuff. He doesn't know what I turned up and until he does there's no point in spending any more time on the project. He could shut down the whole thing."

"That's good, I agree, but what if when you meet with him he's got his big goon Carl with him? That guy scares the shit out of me."

"That's why I'm glad we'll be meeting at Wade's house. I'm guessing there will be all kinds of people around and that should keep things calm. At this point I don't know if Carl told him that he called me and told me to stop talking to the wrong people. Wade 's been real concerned about that damn list. As far as Carl is concerned I'll ask Wade to meet with me alone so there are no distractions."

"Do you think he'll listen?"

"He has to listen. He's our client and he's in charge but we have an obligation to tell the truth. He told me right to my face that he wanted a truthful depiction of his life. He figured he could steer things enough to avoid the whole truth but I won't be part of something that only tells half the story. And he knows we still have to do a bunch of hours of personal interviews with him. I don't think his ego will let him say no."

Saul dropped down into the chair in front of my desk. "Okay, I guess all we can do now is wait and see what he says. It's his move." His voice sounded less than enthusiastic.

"I agree. He sent me an email yesterday that he was done working in the studio fine tuning the concert recording and was heading back to Nashville. He didn't mention anything about Carl's call to me but I know that conversation is coming. When I left him my voicemail I asked if he could stop in Albuquerque on his way but since I didn't hear back from him I'm guessing he's heading straight back to Nashville."

"So that means you'll have to meet him there."

"Yeah, I'm afraid so."

Saul was staring up at the ceiling and after a moment let out a deep sigh and grumbled, "Shit, I think I'd better go too."

Face Time

Saul and I had mixed feelings about going back to Nashville. The circumstances were anything but ideal. He had wanted a return trip to see Lana and a possible escalation of their budding relationship. I'd been looking forward to sharing a total tourist-type of visit with Katie. She wasn't the least bit conflicted about the trip though. Given Carl's ominous phone warning and the troubling history behind Wade's career she wanted me to stay home and tell Wade I wasn't going to work under a threat like that. My decision wasn't that simple. I had never walked away from a project and despite the situation I didn't want to start with this one.

Despite my evening-long efforts to convince Katie that I wasn't at risk of any harm she didn't buy it. Truth be told I was having a little trouble with it myself. I was counting on being in Wade's mansion surrounded by his staff and the usual entourage of hangers-on. It was a very uncomfortable goodbye at our front door the next morning when Saul picked me up. The plan was to make a quick overnight trip to meet for a few hours with Wade and no one else. Our leverage would come from the fact that we'd pulled together some great video and interviews and already had a structure for telling his story. I even had a completed outline that would serve as the backbone of the script. We hoped that when Wade saw what we'd already accomplished he'd be too excited to take a hard line against talking about the other family issues. We knew there was no guarantee.

Saul had been quiet and lost in thought on the plane and as we waited for our Uber to Wade's place he seemed nervous. "You okay?" I asked.

He shrugged. "I guess so, kind of mixed emotions going on. How about you, have you figured out a way to bring up the whole Dixie Mafia subject?"

Yeah, I was thinking I'd come at it from an angle, not just hit him square on with it. I'm going to compare his life to a Country song, you know talk about the trouble and heartache and how people love that shit and why his story has to have that in it."

"What pain and heartache? That guy has lived a charmed life."

"I know but I have the time on the drive to his house to come up with something." My words didn't comfort me any more than they did Saul.

When the driver pulled up to the curb we stashed our bags in the trunk and climbed into the back seat. He said his name was Jason and when I handed him my handwritten information with the address his eyes widened. "Is something the matter?" I asked.

He turned toward me. "Wow, this is up in Belle Meade!"

That meant nothing to me so I asked, "And is that a problem?"

"No it's not a problem it's just the part of town where, well, it's where the rich folks live, like the superstars and celebrities."

"Yeah, that's Wade Teller's address." I waited for his reaction and it was exactly what I'd expected.

"Holy cow, you want me to take you to Wade's place. I've always wondered what it's like. I've only seen pictures."

I smiled and nodded. "Well, Jason, put it in gear and we'll all find out together."

The first twenty minutes were through highway traffic then another fifteen through residential streets. Jason's Honda CRV was barely big enough for the three of us and our baggage but it was comfortable. He seemed to enjoy driving it fast. When the road climbed into rolling hills and farmland he said that we were getting close. Wade called his estate Hill Haven and when we got our first glimpse of it through an opening in the trees there was silence until Saul muttered, "Holy shit." The huge Antebellum-style stone structure was graced with white columns and four large dormers on the slate roof. It looked like something out of a Civil War movie. We pulled into a curving brick drive that passed through an opening in a long stone wall. We stopped at a small guard house beside a large iron gate. Clearly, Hill Haven was well secured. Jason opened his window and we waited for the guard to approach us. For as laid back and down to earth as Wade was it was a totally different vibe outside of his magnificent estate.

The guard stopped a few feet from the car and bent slightly as he looked us over. "Can I help you gentlemen?" He seemed friendly enough and I couldn't help but feel relieved that we hadn't encountered another Carl.

I called out from the backseat, "Yes, we have an appointment with Wade. Jay Rorbach and Saul Worth."

He looked at his phone screen, scrolled for a moment then said, "Yeah, okay, here you are, looks like you're right on time. You can pull in over there under the porte cochere."

Jason turned toward me and asked, "Want me to wait for you?" His expression indicated he wanted me to say yes.

"No thanks, I'm not sure how long we'll be but I'll call you when we're ready to head back to the airport. Sound good?"

There was disappointment in his voice. "Yeah, that's cool. I'll hang around some place close."

We pulled ahead and stopped at the curb under the elegant roof. Before we got out of the car I texted Wade that we'd arrived and he must have been waiting for it because within seconds he replied, "Great, I'll be right out."

Jason helped us pull our bags from the trunk and I followed Saul to the front door. We both scanned the area for any sign of other people, particularly Carl. The front door opened just as we reached it. Wade practically burst through the doorway, grinning widely, and said, "Hey, guys, glad you could make it." We all traded handshakes and I noticed that Wade was looking at the car and Jason. I quickly said, "That's Jason, our Uber driver. He'll be back later to pick us up."

"No, I think he oughta stick around." He walked toward the car and Jason was starry-eyed when Wade offered his hand. Wade stepped back from the car and motioned. "Jason, why don't you just park over by that tree and I'll call down to Dave, my car guy. See that buildin' down the hill there? That's my garage where I keep my car collection. You'd probably enjoy seein' things."

The garage had been built to mimic the main house and from what I could tell from the size and number of overhead doors it looked like it could hold a dozen or more cars. I watched Jason park the car and I was glad he'd be occupied while Saul and I were busy with Wade.

Saul had his video camera going and we were just a few steps inside the door when I felt overwhelmed by the elegance of Hill Haven. I didn't know all of the correct architectural terms to describe the place but it definitely reminded me of *Gone With the Wind*. Wade noticed us staring at every detail and said, "I know it's pretty fancy but I only use the back part of the house. It's where I can let my hair down and be myself." He led us down a long hallway and through a pair of large, rustic oak doors. It was as though we'd entered a different house. We were in a huge room with a beamed ceiling and lined with windows overlooking the back of the property.

Saul stood at the windows with his camera, capturing the view of the huge pool flanked by a brick patio and a fireplace. Beyond it was a large, stone barn and fenced-in pasture with grazing horses. Closer to the main house was another stone building with a small metal sign over the door that read "Studio – No Admittance". It all looked exactly like what it was, the compound of a very wealthy cowboy. "This is where I really live, back here," Wade declared. "I can be myself where it's not so, you know, formal."

I understood exactly what he meant. "I have to say, Wade, this part of the house looks a lot more like your public image, the cowboy with a guitar." Saul smiled and added, "If I lived here I'd never use the front door."

Wade nodded. "Back when Bernie was talkin' me into buyin' the place I told him I'd only do it if I could figure out how to make it a ranch and not a mansion. He just looked at it like an investment not a home. He's a money-first kinda guy. He just works on the numbers and tells me not to ask questions or worry. But I wanted a place where I could be me." He stopped talking when his phone chimed and he looked at the screen. He looked over at Saul, winked and said, "Well, Lana just pulled up out front. She called me this mornin' and asked if she could join us. I didn't think you'd mind."

Saul just smiled and said, "Not at all."

One of the best gauges of the seriousness of a relationship is kiss duration. When Lana walked in and saw Saul their lingering embrace and long, deep kiss told everyone that they had the real thing going on.

For the next hour and a half what had begun as a guided tour of Wade's impressive home slowly turned into an interview in motion. Saul and Lana went on ahead to tape the interior of the house and then went outside to capture the Western flavor of the property. I tried to keep Wade on topic with questions about the house but he had a tendency to go off on tangents about all kinds of subjects. We also had to navigate the household staff and their activities. Even our time outdoors was interrupted by the grounds keeping crew. I hoped that when we went back and reviewed the tape it would be sane enough to fix with some editing. When we'd finally visited every nook and cranny, room, hallway and outdoor space and Saul and Lana had made their way back indoors I said, "Okay, Wade, I'm sure you've been chomping at the bit to see what we've been working on for the past few weeks. Saul, let's put it up on that big flat-screen over there." "Hell no," Wade interrupted. "I got myself a home theater, let's watch it in there."

We all made our way down the hallway again. Everyone found a place to sit and for the next hour and a half we presented the photographs, the unedited video, the interviews and most of the voice-over that would be the core of the documentary.

Between explaining the high points and fielding questions I kept my eyes focused on Wade. His expressions changed back and forth between nostalgic interest and outright glee as his life story unfolded. Admittedly it was just the fun, upbeat part of his story. I'd purposely left out the references and photos related to his family's dark history with the Dixie Mafia. I knew that part would be difficult, even painful, for him to deal with. When the video was over Wade was grinning. "Man that was really somethin', really good stuff."

I knew I had to say something to bring him back to the reality of what the documentary would have to say. "I'm glad you liked it but it's not the whole story and I think you know that. How about we sit on the patio now and really get into the interview we came here to do

Wade nodded and sighed, "Okay." With that one word his upbeat mood seemed to have changed.

While Wade settled into his favorite chair Saul set up the camera and tripod. When it was in place I turned it on and sat down beside it. I looked Wade straight in the eye and said. "Okay, let's talk about the last sixty plus years."

Meanwhile

"I still think we should just walk in there and find out what's goin' on. Sittin' here in a car starin' at Wade's front door is just plain nuts."

"Carl, I know you're not shy about confrontation, sometimes I think you actually enjoy it, but this is one of those situations that we have to handle my way, with a little finesse."

"Look, Bernie, this isn't some kind of god-damned business deal. Those guys could ruin things for both of us, for all of us."

"Calm down. We still don't know what all they found out. They're not detectives they're just a history writer and a video guy. There's no reason to panic."

"When I first heard Wade talkin' about wantin' a show about himself I smelled trouble. That's why I want to go in there and ask those guys face to face what they're goin' to say about Wade's family and all the other folks. I have to find out. I have names to protect in all this. I got people watchin' me."

"I know, some of them are the same people behind *Limelight* and they want to stay invisible too. We all do. There's not much information out there, just the website, and Rorbach isn't going to find out anything by looking at it. Besides, you have to keep in mind that Wade is in there and he'll hear anything we say to those guys. He'll wonder why we care so much about their project. We can't let him know anything about our operation."

"Yeah, and I wonder if he's still nervous about things like he was when we first started explainin' what might go wrong. There's so much shit he doesn't know about and it has to stay that way. And it's all that shit he doesn't know that could hit the fan with this fuckin' documentary of his. I thought my call to Rorbach would scare him off but the guy's in there and I know he's still pressin' Wade for some more stuff about his family."

"Jesus Christ, Carl, why would the guy want to get into the dirt here? He's got no reason to make trouble for Wade,"

"Look, Bernie, all that documentary has to do is drop a few hints about Grampa Earl and Uncle Sonny and people will be off and runnin' about crimes and bad guys and all kinds of mob shit. It'll be all over the internet the next day. They can't find out the real Grampa story. If they do it will lead straight to us. Wade doesn't need to know anything but what we want him to know. Every damn thing we worked for can come crashin' down on us."

"Okay, I agree with you on that part, I just don't want to jump the gun on things. We know they're still working on the project and from what Wade told me he gets first crack at making changes before it's finished. When I put the contact list together for him he didn't object to any of the names."

"It's not the names on the list I'm worried about it's the names that aren't on it, the ones we can't let Wade know about."

"The list isn't the only thing we have to worry about. That's Lana's car sitting over there and she's sweet on that photographer. Who knows what she might have already told him?"

"That's just great, another person we gotta' worry about"

"The guard said they got here about two hours ago. It can't take that much longer to finish the interview so let's just leave and come back later when those guys are gone. We can watch and wait somewhere else."

"Bernie, I'll be watchin' but I can't guarantee I can wait much longer."

Are You Sure
About That?

I'd been thinking about this interview for weeks but as I sat there looking at Wade I had no idea how to start it. The notes I'd written and edited and rewritten suddenly seemed inadequate. It was finally time to decide what the Wade Teller story would be...or wouldn't be.

I cleared my throat and started. "You know, Wade, a couple of weeks ago you asked me if I'd come up with a title for the documentary. I didn't have one then but I think I do now."

His eyes seemed to light up. "Let's hear it!"

"What do you think of *Wade Teller Side B*?

"Hmm, you mean like the B side of a record?"

"Exactly. Everyone knows your Side A. They know your hits and your concerts and all of the stuff they've read in the paper and the magazines over the years. But I don't think they know what's on Side B, the side that's waiting to be listened to after Side A is over."

"Well, the B side's usually not as good as the A side. Some people think of it as a throwaway just to fill the space. The A side is what the fans wanna' hear."

I hesitated, searching for the right words like a salesman ready to make a pitch. "Wade, your fans want to hear anything and everything about you. There's no question that those crowds in the stands are there because they love your music and they love you. They see you in the songs you sing, an imperfect man dealing with love and loss and all the things they deal with in their own lives."

My words seemed to register with him. The faint smile on his face slowly grew and he said, "I gotta admit the part about bein' imperfect sure is true."

"And that's the bond people have with you. The show biz stuff is just the fun part, the Side A. But that doesn't really tell your story. There's a whole lot more to your story than concerts and publicity can tell. That's what Side B is for."

Wade leaned back and stared at the ceiling, rubbing his chin and saying nothing. I didn't want to push him too hard so I just sat and waited. Finally he turned to me and said, "Okay, I like it. Let's go."

Saul and Lana sensed it was time to leave the room and stood up. Saul said, "You don't need me or need us for this part so we'll just go inside for a while. Text me if you need anything."

I waited a moment for them to get through the back door and then switched on the video camera. I quickly scanned my notes and began, "Okay, you started your singing career at a very young age. When other kids were going to high school football games you were singing in clubs. What was it like for you back then?"

Wade had a smile on his face the entire time he talked about his early career. He remembered being nervous in smoky rooms full of adults and seeing things like stumbling drunks and loose women, about the fake I.D. that helped him get free beer from bartenders who pretended it was real. He talked about how long it took for his fingers to get enough calluses that he could stop playing his guitar with a pick. I kept my questions and our conversation focused on him and the music. The longer he talked the more relaxed he became. It was a good story he was telling but when I flipped to page two of my notes I knew the story was about to change direction.

"I saw the old photographs you let us use, the ones of you when you barely needed to shave. The ones when you sang in the church youth choir. And there were some great shots of you and your guitar and the Western outfits. Tell me, how did your family afford all of that? I mean, with you and your brother and sisters needing all of the things kids need?"

Wade looked nervous and I could tell he was searching for his words. "Ah, well let's just say I was lucky to have people in my life that saw somethin' in me, somethin' they were willin' to help me with."

I could have left his answer hang there and move on but doing that wouldn't tell Wade's real story. I nodded and asked, "You mean like your grandfather, Grampa Earl Rollins and your Uncle Sonny Walsh?" There it was, out in the open, the camera was rolling and Wade had to say something. For the first time I was nervous.

Wade sat silently, looking at the floor. He nodded and answered without looking up, "Yeah, they gave me a lot, pretty much everythin' I needed. My Dad was gone and my Mom didn't have much so I was glad they backed me." He paused then added, "But there were other people that helped me, we should talk about them too." He didn't say which people he had in mind but it was obvious he wanted to steer the conversation away from Grampa Earl.

I knew I had to be careful. I couldn't risk spooking him or pissing him off. "Oh, I know you had a lot of help. We talked to your family and some of your old friends. They all said you had lots of support." I waited for his reaction but all I got was a slight smile and a nod. I continued, "The reason I'm curious about your grandfather is that he seemed like the one who poured a lot of money and, well, let's call it influence into your career."

Wade's nervousness was more noticeable. "Well, yeah, that's true. I guess you could say Grampa was my biggest fan. I still have that old Martin guitar he bought me. It's hangin' on the wall downtown at Tootsie's."

"Yeah, I saw it on the Wall of Fame, very cool, but it wasn't just the guitar, it was the years of his influencing people on your behalf. When I was digging into your story I learned how he spent years making sure people gave you work and your Uncle Sonny did the same thing. Those two sure had a lot of power in certain circles." I waited to see if the "certain circles" comment caused a reaction. It did.

"Jay, how about we take a little break here. I need to take a leak and make a phone call. Let's say ten minutes tops."

All I could think was that I'd just pushed the wrong button and it spooked him. And I wondered who he had to call so urgently. "Okay, do what you gotta do and I'll wait here." After the door closed behind him I exchanged texts with Jason and he was fine with waiting a little longer for us to wrap up things.

Ten minutes turned to twenty and wherever he was making his call he was out of earshot. The longer I waited the more certain I was that he was nervous. Another ten minutes went by and I started to wonder if the interview was in jeopardy. When Wade finally came back out on to the patio I waited and tried to gauge his expression.

"Sorry, man, my call took longer than I figured." He dropped back on to his chair but it was clear that his earlier enthusiasm for our conversation had all but disappeared.

It was time to get to the point. "Look, Wade, it's been a great few weeks and Saul and I think we have the makings of a documentary we can all be proud of, and that includes you." His expression brightened but only a little. "Just like when we worked on Encino every one of these projects I've worked on has brought a few surprises. It just sort of goes with the territory. And I think you know we found a few surprises in your story too."

He nodded. "You mean Grampa."

"That's right, Grampa Earl and Uncle Sonny too."

"Is the camera runnin' right now?"

"Yeah, do you want me to turn it off?"

There was a long silence and then, "No, I guess we should talk about all this."

I had no sooner checked to make sure Wade's image was centered on the camera screen when Saul walked out to join us. He was grinning ear to ear but when he saw Wade's rigid expression and my serious look he picked up on the vibe. "Sorry, guys. Lana's headed home and I know I need to help finish things up here." He dragged a chair over beside mine and sat down. I figured that he'd quickly picked up on the reason for the more somber feeling to the interview so I started back in with my questions.

"Wade, remember when I told you about the whole Side B thing as the title for the project? I said your fans all know about problems and dark things in their own lives. They're not perfect people and they don't expect you to be perfect either. They won't be surprised to find out about things from the past that aren't all perfect and warm and fuzzy.'"

Wade was looking right into the camera, right into his fans' eyes. "Yeah, I suppose so."

"So let's talk a little about your Grampa and your Uncle, about their involvement in your career."

For the next half hour Wade did most of the talking, spinning stories about growing up with his grandfather as a constant part of his life. He talked about his mother's embarrassment when Grampa got into trouble and how it sometimes brought her to tears. It was as though Grampa had two distinct personalities and the family never knew which one would walk through the door. But he was also a kind of father substitute that Wade needed at that age. He smiled when he told about the Saturday afternoon when Grampa walked the seventeen-year-old Wade into a small nightclub called *Percy's* and within half an hour made a deal for Wade to perform for more money than he'd ever imagined. There was no audition even though Wade had his guitar with him. It had been a closed-door meeting between Grampa and Percy while Wade sat in a booth and waited. He described the expression on Percy's face when the meeting was over as total bewilderment. Whatever was said in that room led to Wade getting his first professional gig. When he was finished with the story Wade looked at me then at Saul and muttered, "Damn, Grampa was somethin' else."

I looked over my notes to see where I wanted the conversation to go next then Wade asked, "Hey, man, do we have to use that story? I mean, what if it makes people think Grampa was a bad guy?"

I knew I had to be honest with him. "Wade, in a way your grandfather *was* a bad guy, but I think there's been some real exaggeration of the things he did." He gave a slight nod as I reached over and turned off the camera. "Wade, since all of this stuff came about from my research we never really got to talk about it. Let me ask you, who all knows about Grampa and Uncle Sonny and their past?"

It took Wade awhile to answer but finally he said, "It's hard to say. At first it was just the family. But then Grampa got arrested and it was all over town, and a few days later Uncle Sonny got nabbed too." There was another very long silence before he added, "My Momma didn't stop cryin' for a whole week." Another long pause and then, "Hell, I've been pretendin' that it's no big deal but I guess everyone knows about it."

It was clear that Wade was troubled by the subject and I was reluctant to push him too hard. But I knew it could be a critical part of the story. Without asking him I turned the camera back on. I looked over at Saul and he gave a slight nod toward Wade as if saying, "Keep it going."

That's Enough

"Come on, Carl, get back in the car."

No, I've had it. No more waitin'."

"It looks like maybe things are wrapping up. Lana's car is gone but the Uber driver's car is still down at the garage. It looks like whether we like it or not we're still in a holding pattern."

"Bullshit! The longer they're all in there the worse this is all goin' to turn out."

"Keep in mind that we work for Wade and he's in charge here. His house, his rules. Get back in the god-damned car."

"When I tell him what that Rorbach is diggin' into he'll agree with me."

"All you're going to do is make him wonder why we're so concerned about it. He has no idea how much or how little we know about what Rorbach might have found out and if we go barging in there we'll just give ourselves away. Now get back into the car and we'll come back later."

"Look, Bernie, you're makin' a whole lot more off of Wade than I am. You got your sweet deal with the partners but all I got is a monthly check and nothin' else. There's no way in hell I'm gonna let somebody make me go broke from all this"

"Just stop for a second. Let's play this one out in our heads before we do anything. Wade's in there and I'm sure there are a few staff people running around. Rorbach and the photographer are probably sitting with Wade. That's a lot of eyes and ears that could take in every word and action. That means there's a lot of risk involved no matter what. Are you sure you want to barge in there and take that kind of chance?"

"Okay, I get it. It's a damned if we do and damned if we don't, at least that's how I see it. You know I was never good at sittin' on my ass and watchin' things happen, I always want to be in the middle of things."

"And I know from experience that there were times when you kicked some ass that didn't need to be kicked and it caused trouble for Wade."

"I was just doin' my job. That's what a security guy does."

"You and I have a totally different take on what *security* means. I still say waiting a little longer can't hurt."

"Sorry, Bernie, we've done it your way long enough. It's time the Head of Security does his job."

What's the Real Deal?

We gave Wade the time he needed to collect himself. Finally, he sat up straight in his chair, cleared his throat and said, "Sorry, guys, I haven't talked about this stuff for a hell of a long time. Let's go, keep the camera rolling."

The sound of people in the hallway interrupted us. Millie, Wade's head housekeeper came rushing into the room. "I'm so sorry, Wade. I told these boys you were busy and couldn't be bothered but, as usual, the big goon there wouldn't listen."

Carl glared at her. "This doesn't concern her, Wade, would you ask her to leave please?"

Wade stood up, clearly agitated. "It's okay, Millie, I got this." He waited for her to leave and then said, "You guys could have called me instead of comin' in here unannounced. We're busy with the documentary stuff."

Bernie stepped in front of Carl, trying to get control of the situation. "I'm sorry, Wade, this was all Carl's idea and we'll just get on out of here. We can talk later."

Carl put a big hand on Bernie's shoulder and pushed him aside, his glare now aimed at me. The only thing making me feel safe was that Wade was right beside me and I figured, more like hoped, that he could keep Carl under control. Since the interview had been my idea and my project I looked Carl square in the eye and said, "This is a personal interview with Wade and no one else. The documentary is about him and we'd like you to leave now. We'll be finished in half an hour or so." I looked over at Saul and saw the color had drained from his face. He kept his gaze on Wade to see what might happen next.

Carl wasn't the brightest man but even he could read the room. He leaned toward me and snarled, "Look, Rorbach, this isn't over. Just remember what I told you on the phone."

"And what exactly did you tell him on the phone?" Wade asked. He was clearly upset with his self-named Chief of Security.

Before Carl could answer him I said, "He told me I wasn't just working for you, that I'm working for him and Bernie too, and that I shouldn't talk to anyone who isn't on the list you gave me."

"Carl, what makes you think these guys are workin' for you and Bernie? Is there somethin' goin' on here I don't know about?"

At that moment Bernie was the perfect example of "if looks could kill". He grabbed Carl's sleeve. "God dammit, Carl, I told you not to say anything!" It wasn't exactly a denial of Carl's comments but more of an "I agree but let's just wait until later to say anything else". He tugged on Carl's arm and turned to leave. "Sorry, Wade, I'll call you later."

I saw an opportunity that I might not get again. I took a deep breath and said, "Wait a second, Bernie, I just had one quick question for you. If I need anything more can I stop by your office and talk to one of your *partners*?" I used very large, almost mocking air-quotes around the word "partners". The uncomfortable look on Bernie's face was obvious and I noticed Saul was smirking. Bernie didn't answer me and the two men hurried out of the room and down the hallway. Mollie followed them as if to make sure they actually left the house.

The three of us looked at each other and I was sure that we shared the same feeling of relief. After we all sat down again Wade asked, "Did you get that on the video because it was kind of embarrassin' to have my people actin' like that."

"Yeah, I got the whole thing but don't worry, it won't be in the final cut."

Saul leaned toward me and asked, "What were those air-quotes all about when you said the word partners?"

"Yeah, Jay, I was wonderin' that myself."

There was no way to avoid the topic any longer. "Well, how do I say this? Um, like I told you before, while I was doing my normal research, things like old newspaper archives, public records and online searches I turned up a few surprises. That was how I found out about Grampa and Sonny." I saw the stories about their criminal histories but you know, something just didn't smell right to me. The stuff they were arrested for was minor stuff; small scale thefts and break-ins. They weren't angels but they weren't hardened criminals either."

Wade looked puzzled. "The way I heard it from Carl and Bernie, Grampa was a bad ass and everyone was scared to death of him. Sonny too."

"That's what they wanted you to believe. There's a hell of a lot more to this story, your story, than meets the eye. I read everything I could find on your family and I also did some digging into Carl and Bernie. It might sound like I'm playing detective here but I reached a conclusion that I want to run by you."

Saul had the same puzzled look as Wade had and asked, "It sounds like your saying that Grampa wasn't the only bad ass in this story."

"No, I'm saying Grampa wasn't a bad ass at all. Bernie and Carl have painted a picture of a vicious and dangerous old man that simply didn't exist. Old Grampa Earl had his share of run-ins with the law but in the end it turned out to be pretty trivial stuff. Did you know he never served more than thirty days in jail for any of the things he did? That's hardly what you'd call a dangerous man."

"Then why would Bernie and Carl come up with that list of people for you to talk to and say not to ask questions about Grampa? They told me you guys would just use that stuff to make trouble and confuse things."

It was time to drop my bomb. I took a deep breath and started. "Wade, here's my take on things. In the world of magic the magician uses what's called misdirection. He gets people focused on one thing while he's messing around with another thing and they don't see what he's doing. Bernie and Carl have been doing that to you. They got you so worried about Grampa messing up your story that they knew you wouldn't see what they've been up to."

"What do you mean? What are they doing?

"Okay, keep in mind that this is only my take on things based on the digging I've done so far. I first got suspicious when I started looking into Limelight Partners. It looks like there aren't any partners, at least not any that actually work. Bernie appears to be the whole show, like he works by himself. There's just a ridiculously lame website and they don't even have anyone to answer the phone. You get a recording of a woman's voice asking you to leave a message."

Wade shook his head. "I don't get it. Why is that a problem?"

"Don't you think a firm that claims to represent high-powered talent like you would also brag that they represent other big names? There's nothing on their website or anywhere else that says that. Wade, years ago when you were young you put your career and income in Bernie's hands. You've made a lot of money but have you ever asked him for the details, I mean like how much and where it all goes?"

"He gives me regular reports. I see how much I made and the accounts I have."

"And do you think it's all there? Do you think one guy can possibly handle everything by himself?"

"I never really thought about it. There's always money in the bank and I'm always so damn busy I just leave it all to Bernie to handle. What kind of problem are you seein' that I'm not?"

"I want to be clear here. I'm not trying to make trouble for you or anyone, but I started all of this research to get to know you and to learn why Wade Teller is the man that he is. What I found was kind of a puzzle. I found a huge, money making machine called The Wade Teller Band. It's the kind of operation that needs a whole team of people to run the business but supposedly one man handles it all. Limelight Partners is a smokescreen. It's meant to fool you into feeling you're in good hands, a lot of hands. I paused for a moment then added, "And when I asked a few questions about your past and who helped you back then and who helps you now I was told very strongly to shut up and stay away from it."

Saul chimed in, "I think I get it. It's Bernie and Carl using misdirection. Turn Grampa into some kind of villain and while you're focusing on him and thinking you have to hide him. Grampa is what you have to worry about. Meanwhile, they're busy doing things they don't want you or anyone else to notice. And they have help doing them."

I nodded. "You got it! They knew that if we looked into Grampa and Sonny we just might find out other things too, like the fake management business."

Wade still looked confused so I gave him a little time for things to sink in. When he still didn't respond I said, "Wade, I think the story of Grampa can be a beautiful part of the documentary, a little colorful maybe but also very surprising and very touching. He loved you and you loved him despite his faults. I think your fans will love him too."

Wade nodded and seemed to be more relaxed. "After all these years I still miss him. Grampa was kind of a rogue but people really liked bein' around him."

"I think the viewers will too."

Saul chimed in. "So what about Bernie and Carl? They're really pissed off and I have a feeling we haven't heard the last from them."

Wade stood up. "Don't you worry about those boys, they're my problem and I'll handle it."

It seemed like a good time to wrap things up so Saul and I stood up and began packing the equipment. "Wade, we really appreciate all of the time you've given us. I know we've thrown you a few curveballs and it's probably not what you were expecting from us. Remember when we talked about the Encino documentary and the importance of honesty with those people? That's what made that story special and I think your honesty about Grampa will make your story special too."

Wade was finally smiling again and when I reached for a handshake I got a bear hug instead. "Thanks, Jay. Thanks, Saul. I have a much better feelin' about the whole thing now."

Saul also got a bear hug along with a little advice. "Lana's a good person, a little high-strung sometimes but you be patient and hang in there with her, okay?"

Saul grinned. "Don't worry, man, I'm hanging in and hanging on."

Are We There Yet?

I texted Jason to pick us up under the port cochere, hoping he wasn't upset that we'd kept him waiting for so long. Wade walked us out and stood with us while we waited. When the car pulled up I was surprised at the smile on Jason's face. He popped open the trunk and then stepped out and headed straight for Wade. "Man, your collection is amazing. The XK-150 is beautiful but that Shelby Cobra is my favorite."

Wade smiled. "Mine too, a little man, glad you enjoyed yourself." He patiently allowed Jason to take a selfie with him.

We said our goodbyes and I promised Wade that we'd have a good, mostly polished video for him to review within a few weeks. Minutes later we were pulling on to the main road when Saul said, "Oh great, I think that's Carl in that car back there."

I turned to look. "And it looks like he's going to follow us. Shit."

Jason looked in the rearview mirror. "I don't know who Carl is but he sounds like a problem' Want me to lose him?" I wasn't sure how to answer him. He smiled and said, "Remember? I'm a driver, it's what I do." He accelerated quickly and Carl did the same. "Don't worry, guys, I know what I'm doing."

My first reaction was to tell him to slow down and drive like an Uber driver was supposed to drive but when Carl got close enough for me to see his face I just tugged on my seatbelt and stayed silent. High speed car chases weren't a part of a historian's work routine but then nothing about this assignment had been routine. I looked at Jason and he was clearly enjoying himself but I was sure that high speed chases weren't a part of an Uber driver's life either.

It was a white knuckle drive on an unfamiliar highway. Shifting my gaze back and forth between Carl behind us and the winding road in front of us I said, "Jason, there's no reason for the speed. That guy can't do anything as long as our car is moving, even slowly. How about slowing down? This CRV isn't exactly made for competitive driving."

Jason backed off the gas pedal a litle and I could see the relief on Saul's face. That look lasted until Carl's front bumper made hard contact with our rear bumper. Jason sped up slightly and Carl did the same, hitting our bumper again. That was Jason's breaking point. He muttered, "Okay, asshole, let's see what you can do." Before I could say anything we were back up near sixty-five and I held my breath when I saw a tight curve ahead. "Don't worry," Jason said, "I got this." We went into the curve and Jason expertly maintained control while barely slowing down. Carl wasn't so skillful. I watched as he over-corrected and fishtailed before sliding sideways into a deep, muddy culvert. Before we got out of view I saw him pounding his fists on the steering wheel. Poor Carl wasn't going any farther.

I finally exhaled. "Okay, Jason, it's over. Let's get to the airport the normal way now." I heard him mutter under his breath, "That was so cool."

It was an easy flight to Dallas but our connecting flight to Albuquerque was delayed. We found a bar near our gate and waited. Saul had been quiet on the plane and that didn't change as we sat there. "Are you okay?" I asked him.

"Yeah, I guess so. I just have a lot going on in my head."

"We knew this was going to be a different kind of project."

"Different doesn't begin to describe it. There was the naïve client, the shady businessman and the big, scary thug."

"And a beautiful woman who's crazy about you."

He shrugged and nodded. "I admit, she's the only reason I went back to Nashville with you."

"I know that. Thanks for being there. It wasn't easy for me either."

"So what happens next? It seems like we're pretty much finished getting all the information and we're ready to make the finished product. Am I reading it right?""

"Yeah, I think we're pretty much there. I have a lot of writing to do and you have a ton of images and video to edit. We're both gonna be buried for a while before we get together for the final push."

"I don't know about you but when we left Wade's house I felt like we left him hanging, I mean with all that trouble with Bernie and Carl."

"I know, I feel the same way. He's such a nice guy but gullible as hell when it comes to people and his finances. He's made a whole lot of money but I have a feeling Bernie and his so-called partners have made even more. And as for Carl, with no more touring involved he's pretty much useless to Wade." I glanced over at the large flight monitor near the bar and saw that our flight was finally boarding. "We better get going. I can't wait to get home." Saul didn't respond and I could tell that his mind was still back in Nashville.

The flight was a little bumpy and we landed in a light rain. Katie was waiting at the arrival pick-up and I'm sure she wondered why I hugged her a little harder and longer than usual. Saul did a good job of acting like nothing was wrong until Katie asked him about Lana. He didn't say much but it was obvious that she was at the front of his thoughts. When we got to my house he left quickly.

Katie had Chinese take-out waiting and we spent the evening catching up with each other. I was open and honest about everything that had happened and she was as relieved as I was that the project would be completed in Albuquerque. She knew the process I followed and what to expect in the weeks ahead. What neither of us had an answer to was how we could help Wade with his personnel problems but I knew I had to come up with something. At that point I wasn't sure if I'd created his problem or just revealed it. Either way I wanted to help him.

Side B, the Hard Way

My years of doing research had taught me how to identify, analyze and solve problems. I'd also learned the value of talking to people with expertise that I didn't have. Wade had a business problem and that was not in my wheelhouse. Charlie Hamlin had been handling my accounting and tax work for a long time so he seemed like a perfect starting point. While I was on hold with his office I tried to figure out how to explain Wade's problem and how I had gotten involved, and do it without revealing any names.

Our conversation asked as many questions as it answered but I managed to glean some great information and suggestions for Wade. From his end all he was expecting from me was a finished documentary but I owed him more than that. When I called him on the phone I fully expected some confusion.

"Hey, Jay, good to hear from you, didn't expect a call so soon."

"Neither did I. We're working hard on the final editing and things are looking really good but there's something else I need to talk to you about."

"What's that?"

"Well, I kind of feel like I owe you an apology. That whole thing with Carl and Bernie wasn't anything I planned or wanted to get involved in. But from the start of the project we agreed that trust was important and that's why I'm calling."

There was silence before he replied, "Not sure I follow."

"I guess the best thing to do here is to be totally blunt. First, when we left your house yesterday Carl followed us and tried to run us off the road. He's trying to hide something. What it is I'm not sure but he's really

---

113

sweating something. Second, I think you should check out Bernie and his so-called partners. I have a gut feeling his partners are mob-connected and you've been their cash cow all these years. They think our story is going to expose them. You sure don't need that kind of shit in your life." I figured that was enough to lay out for him and just waited for his response.

"Well, man, I'm sorry about Carl doin' that. He's always been a damn hot head but it didn't bother me when I needed him watchin' over me and the band. I won't be needin' that kind of thing anymore and he knows it. He's probably job-scared."

"That's probably it but be careful getting rid of that guy."

"And as for Bernie, well, I don't really know what to do there. I sure don't know business the way he does. Hell, I wouldn't know where to start."

"I understand but I have an idea that just might give you the help you need. My accountant gave me the names of two what are called forensic accountants. They're guys that can dig into old financial records and sniff out any signs of theft or fraud. One's in Memphis and one's in Atlanta."

"You keep sayin' things about Bernie screwin' me over or somethin'."

"Wade, I don't know the specifics, I only know that his company appears to be fake and that he's had you worrying about people finding out about Grampa. Grampa was never your problem but that's what he wanted you and everyone else to believe so you wouldn't ask questions."

"So these forensic guys can check things out to see if I'm bein' screwed over?"

"Yep, they're the experts on finding that, and if they find that Bernie and his phantom partners did you wrong they'll also give you advice on how to shut them down."

Wade was silent for a while and I knew he was troubled. Finally he said, "Well, okay. I'll reach out to the one in Memphis, it's closer to home. I just hope I get me some answers."

"You will and I think you'll get something even better."

"What's that?"

"You'll get your grandfather back."

For the next few weeks Saul and I were practically joined at the hip trying to finish the project. We felt like we were finally back into our normal state; writing, editing, arguing and watching the story come to life. Even Super-fan Katie joined in the process with her knowledge of the band and their songs. I'd even taken some time to shop the documentary and found a surprising amount of interest from *PBS American Masters* and *Country Music Television*. I anticipated an actual bidding war for the show.

Our final trip to Nashville came with a whole different vibe compared to previous ones. We'd always enjoyed presenting our finished product to the client but we knew this time would be a whole other thing. Katie came along and we planned a few extra days to be tourists in Musicland. My original plan was to call Jason again when we got to the airport but Lana surprised us, waiting at the gate with a huge embrace and kiss for Saul.

During the drive to Wade's house she brought us up to date on what had been happening at their end. One of the accountants I'd recommended to Wade had already uncovered Bernie's scheme to skim extra fees and charges from Wade's accounts. Wade couldn't decide which would be worse for Bernie, facing legal action or simply having to explain to his mob partners why their gravy train was coming to an end. Either way Bernie was screwed.

With no band tours in the future Carl was out of a job. Lana told us about the plight of a man with no marketable skills except his size and bad temper. The best he could do was a job as a bouncer at a nightclub downtown. And, unfortunately, goons don't get a retirement plan.

Wade greeted us at the front door and half an hour later we were settled again into his home theater room for the unveiling of *Wade Teller Side B*. Saul and I were proud of what we'd created but Wade's was the only opinion that counted. In past presentations I'd stood before my clients and given them a brief overview but not this time. This documentary would speak for itself.

Even in the darkened room there was enough light from the screen that I could see Wade's face and his expressions as the scenes changed. His transitions from childhood to teen years to adulthood all carried their own set of emotions but it was the times when Grampa Earl was on the screen that his face gave him away. I could see the tears in his eyes and a faint smile. His grandfather, the real one not the exaggerated bad guy that Bernie had created, was back in Wade's memory the way he belonged. Wade turned and looked at me, not even trying to hide his tears. He nodded, smiled and gave me a thumbs up.

Alive... for Now

Growing Pains

Success is one of the vaguest words in the English language. Sometimes you don't even know if you have it because people define it in so many different ways. Some base it on income or material things. Others base it on the public reaction or adulation their efforts brought about, like being famous. And there are a few people who base it solely on the personal satisfaction that comes from a job well done. As I sat at my desk that morning, three months after our documentary about Wade Teller had premiered, it was clear to me that all three definitions were true.

Wade had reached deep into his pockets for our fees and production costs. *Country Music Television* had outbid *PBS American Masters* for the broadcast rights and had promoted it heavily. The ratings were through the roof and Saul and I were proud of the finished product. There was no doubt in my mind that *Wade Teller Side B* had been a success by any definition.

Despite that success it had been hard to decide on our next project. Saul and I had been talking and at times arguing about the direction to take *Then and Now Productions,* our newly formalized partnership. Truth be told the seduction of working with famous people had really gotten to me just like it had to Saul even though I wouldn't admit it to him. I pretended that all I wanted to do was get back into doing what I knew best, historical themes. We were equal partners on paper but our respective roles and strengths wouldn't be so easy to balance.

When I saw Saul pull into the driveway I knew our little "Come to Jesus" moment was at hand. Knowing that I always made overly strong coffee we sat down with the Starbuck's order he'd picked up, ready to chart the course of our new company.

There was an uncomfortable silence for a moment before Saul broke the ice with, "Did you watch the Lobos game on Saturday?"

It seemed like as good a way as any to get started. "Only the first half. When Texas Tech went up by two touchdowns I couldn't stand to watch anymore."

"The second half was just as ugly. It's looking like it'll be a long season."

I smiled. "Then let's make sure we're so damn busy we won't have time to care."

Saul nodded and sighed. "Yeah, I guess it's time to dig into all of this." He leaned back in his chair, took a long sip of his coffee and looked right at me. "You know, man, we've gotta settle this whole celebrity versus history thing before we can take on any new projects."

"I agree. Neither of us was looking for a music star project but Wade dumped one in our laps and I can't deny it all worked out great. But that doesn't mean we should be pigeon-holing ourselves with celebrity stories only. We got really good at the historical stuff too. It's what we built our resumes on."

"Yeah, I know that but we made more money on Wade than our last three or four projects combined. That's pretty damn hard to ignore. Once you get a taste of that you don't want to give it up. That's me. I don't want to give it up."

I tried hard to keep from showing how much I agreed with him. "I can't argue with that point but I'm an historian."

"I know that but remember what Shakespeare said, "There is a history in all men's lives." So I guess it's all in how you look at it"

"Geez, you're starting to sound like me.

"Look, I agree we shouldn't pigeon hole ourselves but there's gotta be a way we can do both. You can get your History Geek on once in a while and I can do my Photographer to the Stars thing sometimes. There's nothing that says we can't have it both ways."

Saul's willingness to compromise surprised me. It sounded like an easy solution but I knew that actually doing it would be a lot harder to pull off. Juggling serious historical subjects and research with celebrity ego trips would be almost like running two separate businesses. "I've been thinking of that too but I'm not sure we could manage the logistics if we tried to do two different kinds of projects at the same time."

"Okay, so we alternate them. You said you've been putting together a list of project ideas, all the requests and emails you've gotten since Wade's show went live. It's like everyone who's even marginally famous thinks they deserve their own documentary. Let's look at the list and see if there's a way to handle a couple of them."

I set down my coffee and pulled up the list on my laptop screen. "Okay, here they are, in no particular order. Uh, on the celebrity side we have Danny Stewart, the PGA golf star with a big ego and an even bigger drinking and substance abuse problem. He wants us to tell his sad story."

Saul shrugged and shook his head. "Sounds like a head case."

"Yeah, he might be too much of a flake. Another celebrity option is John Upton, the aging record company executive and egomaniac who claims to have discovered almost everyone famous and says he has had affairs with a dozen famous women."

"He sounds like someone I wouldn't want to be in the same room with."

"I agree. How about this one, the life story of Amy Welch, another Country singer? She was referred to us directly by Wade. She's never made it to super-star status, not even close, and I have a feeling she wants us to do a documentary that'll boost her struggling career."

"Nope, that's not what we do. What else have you got?"

I was getting frustrated. Okay, here's one of my historical opportunities. A couple of months ago some very old and very valuable Hopi jewelry and artifacts were discovered in a dry well on an old, abandoned ranch south of Santa Fe. There's some Navajo pottery in the mix too. Some people who so far haven't identified themselves told the newspaper about it. They were nosing around and found it all. The property was once owned by a silent movie producer named James Roessler and had been left to the elements ever since it all burned down in 1947. They never found out how the fire started. Roessler died in the fire. His estate still owns it but it's completely deserted."

"That one sounds interesting, like a historical mystery. Too bad everyone involved is probably dead."

I couldn't help but roll my eyes and smirk. "Yeah, they're dead but the owner was a dead celebrity so it's right up your alley."

Saul gave me the finger and said, "Okay, I get your point."

I had a few more names on my list but it didn't seem like we were getting anywhere. Saul got up to use the bathroom and I sat there scrolling through my notes. Choosing our next project wasn't the only thing I wanted to discuss with him. It was time to look into other media markets and our newly-formed partnership would let us do that. That was a topic I knew we had to chew on soon. When Saul came back in and sat down I said, "You know, we might be looking at these project decisions the wrong way."

"What do you mean?"

"I mean all the things we've done so far have been full-length documentaries for television."

"Yeah, what's your point?"

"My point is I don't think that's always going to be the best format. It makes us construct our story to fit into a specific amount of time. I think we're missing out on a few, I guess you could say, more modern ways to show and sell our work."

"Such as?"

"Such as a Docuseries or a Podcast. I'm sure you and Lana stream shows. Katie and I do it a lot. The serialized format is tailored to people who can't or won't sit and watch or listen to a long story in one viewing. Shows that are streamed get the biggest audiences. If we went that way we'd have to write and edit our stuff in bite-size chunks but I think it'd be worth a try."

Saul was silent for a moment and I couldn't read his expression. Finally he said, "Well, since a Podcast is audio only I'd be pretty much out of a job."

"No, I just mentioned a podcast for reference. We're both visual guys and the video docuseries would be the only way for us to go."

Again there was silence and I gave my friend and partner all the time he needed. He nodded. "You know, I think you're on to something. It would be a lot more work to edit a story in pieces but it would let us make the whole thing longer overall. And easier to sell too. I like it."

"Great, because it's not easy selling a ninety minute or two hour show to anyone these days."

"The celebrity stories you mentioned sound kind of lame but the golfer probably has deep pockets." How do you feel about working with a rich asshole on drugs?"

"I know we could probably make some good money but at what cost?"

"Yeah, it might be too risky getting paid. Let's keep it on the list for now. I guess that one about the dead Hollywood guy and the Indian jewelry could work. It sounds like something right up our alley, both of us."

"I thought the same thing. I don't know all of the details about it yet but if you agree I'll start shopping the concept to a couple of streaming platforms and see if I can get us a client. I'm hoping for some seed money too but we might have to start self-financing our work. Meanwhile you can be checking out some of the streaming shows to see how the editing is handled."

"Seed money would be nice. Wade spoiled us."

We checked our upcoming schedules and wrapped up our meeting. It felt good to have an agenda again after a long hiatus and I was excited about the new direction we were headed. I also felt like a historian again, albeit one who secretly enjoyed the celebrity fluff.

Expect the Unexpected

It didn't take me long to get back into a groove. Doing historical research is in my blood and I'd missed digging into old records and books. While I didn't have to research the entire project I'd have to develop enough of a story outline to make it intriguing enough to shop it to the streaming platforms. That meant I not only had to see the process through the eyes of the viewer but I also had to think like a content creator. I wanted to build the *Then and Now* brand and get the exposure we needed to promote it.

My focus started with *Disney+* and *Netflix*. There were a few specialty platforms that might have been easier but I figured if we were going to go through all of the time and effort we might as well try for the big guys. Saul agreed that our portfolio of projects on the networks gave us the credibility that those big guys would be looking for. Now I had to come up with enough hard information for a solid storyline and sales pitch.

My research had started with the piece of property in question; the old, abandoned Roessler Ranch. After less than an hour of digging into old County maps and property deeds I came across something that gave me a jolt. The ranch was directly on the opposite side of Route 285 from the town limits of Encino, just over a mile from the intersection with Railroad Street and Jack's station. I had driven by it a dozen times but thought it was just open range. The few buildings that had made it a working ranch had been destroyed in a mysterious fire that old newspaper accounts described as "suspicious" and "total and devastating".

A few more hours of digging provided some old black and white photos of the ranch while it was in operation. Old James Roessler had been a notorious publicity hound and cut a wide path in Hollywood society. The newspaper, the *Santa Fe New Mexican* had accumulated numerous photos of him. He had lived in Los Angeles and was quite famous during his movie-making years. His friends included starlets, millionaires and mobsters.

There was a story about how he had alienated the Native American community by using white actors in make-up for his lone Western movie, *Range War*. The handful of men he'd hired to work on the ranch had constant run-ins with the people from the local Navajo reservation. James Roessler was not a popular man in New Mexico. Sadly, he never quite reached his former fame after movies with sound came about. Hollywood lost interest in him and he retired in 1928. He moved to the ranch during the Great Depression.

I was never much of a believer in coincidence but the fact that a new potential project was located so close to a previous one in a big state like New Mexico had me wondering. Given the amount of time between the demise of the ranch and the birth of Encino it was hard to connect the two places. Reluctantly, I decided it was nothing more than, well, a coincidence. When I heard the garage door opening I knew Katie was home and I'd have a chance to think about something else.

I walked into the kitchen just as she came through the door. "Hi, babe, how are things in the wonderful world of healthcare?"

She offered a tired looking smile and shook her head. "Oh, it was one of those days when I think about how I can't wait to retire."

"Problems?"

"Just the usual ones, staff shortage, budget shortage, time shortage. You name it and whatever it is, we need more of it."

"Well, try to put it behind you for the evening. Go in and change your clothes and I'll meet you on the patio."

Fifteen minutes later we clinked our wine glasses and looked out over the high desert and the mountains beyond. It was a beautiful late summer view that never failed to make life feel a little easier to handle. Katie leaned back and asked, "How was your day? Are you any closer to writing the scope of that ranch project?"

"Yeah, I made a little headway on it and I also discovered an interesting little fact. The Roessler Ranch is directly across the road from Encino."

"You're kidding! That's so, I don't know, weirdly coincidental."

There was that word again. "Yeah, I suppose it is but it's just so strange that an abandoned ranch sits so close to an abandoned town and they're two totally separate things."

Her eyes widened. "It's kind of spooky."

"Yeah, there's already so much mystery around the fire at the ranch and the fact that Roessler died alone in it and nobody ever tried to rebuild. No one ever figured out what caused the fire either. From what I could find out so far his son was his only direct, first generation heir and he didn't want the place. He couldn't find a buyer and the estate still owns it. The son died about twenty years ago. His daughter, Roessler's granddaughter, wasn't interested in running the place either but hung on to it. Legally she still owns it and her son handles the estate."

"What about all of the Indian jewelry and artifacts? Who owns that?"

"I haven't dug into the law behind that yet but I'm pretty sure that anything tangible found on the property belongs to the current owner, which is Roessler's estate, his granddaughter. That also begs the question of how the artifacts got into the well."

"It's such a weird story. Someone who so far doesn't want to be identified just happens to discover valuable things in an empty well on an abandoned property and goes public with it. That's more than a coincidence. It doesn't sound like anything but a crime."

I took a long sip of wine and nodded. "I agree, but since no one ever reported the stuff as missing the Sheriff can't really investigate it."

"What about the Hopi?"

"All I've found out about that is there's a tribal spokesman in the Taos Pueblo who wants to examine everything but so far no one from the estate has responded to him. And the finder still hasn't come forward."

"So are you stuck too or can you keep doing your research?"

"Well, I can just work around it for a while but eventually I'll have to tackle it somehow, either through the Sheriff's office or one of the tribes."

I wasn't surprised when her Mother Hen side started to come out. "Making historic documentaries isn't supposed to be dangerous but somehow your last two projects have had a dark side to them. This one sounds like it could be more of the same and I'm not happy about it."

I felt like I was on the defensive but I knew she had a point. And I knew that she only brought it up because she cared about me. "Babe, if anything starts to look dangerous I'll get out."

"You said that during Encino and again with Wade."

"Yeah, I guess I did, but just please trust me not to do anything too risky, okay?"

She tried a weak smile and answered, "I'll believe it when I see it."

Back to Encino

There wasn't much to see on Google and I knew there'd be only so much I would find out in dusty old files and yellowed newspapers. I had to try a "boots on the ground" approach. The Roessler estate had no contact information listed anywhere except for a post office box in Los Angeles. With no other immediate celebrity project option that interested us, Saul had agreed to help me with the search for answers and we headed to the ranch for a closer look.

Saul picked me up in his Jeep because the drone wouldn't fit into my car. Our plan was to pull over on the side of Route 285 somewhere along the fence line of the ranch. All we had for reference was a copy of the land deed with a hand-drawn map from the 1920s. Saul would launch the drone and get aerial photos and video of the place. He'd drop down in altitude to try and get close-up views of the burned out house and barn. We weren't sure of the exact location of the old well so he'd have to do some careful low-altitude snooping. Since the property was unoccupied we assumed there were no restrictions on drone activity but we still planned to keep things as invisible as possible.

The morning drive toward Encino and the ranch felt like old times. There was no scheduling of flights to Nashville, no waiting in airport bars and no using rental cars. It was just the two of us again, working on a story in our home state, enjoying the scenery and easy conversation. It was also a chance for me to catch up on Saul's ever-evolving personal life.

"So how did things go with Lana's interview? Did she get the job?"

"Yeah, she's officially the new keyboardist for Sandia Productions. They've already got her in mind for a bunch of things including a new commercial for U.S. Bank and one for the Tourism Bureau. They're big budget projects and she's pretty excited. They even want her to get involved in writing the music."

"That's great. She must be happy to be working regular hours and not touring and doing night work in bars."

"She's really glad but she's also nervous. We were talking last night and she wondered if she'd be able to handle a normal life."

"I'm sure she'll be fine. Anything is better than never being home." I smiled and added, "Even being home with you." Once again he gave me the finger and a grin.

When we were just a few miles north of Encino, I looked to the east to see if there were any signs of the reopening copper mine. I could see a faint dust cloud in the distance but that was it. "Man, I thought there'd be more signs of progress with the mine but it's just a little dust."

Saul glanced out over the hills. "From what I've been reading in the paper and online American Mining has made all kinds of promises to make things right. They say they've got crews working to get the recommissioning done and make the pit operational again. I haven't seen or heard the details."

"Yeah, that's all well and good for American but it sounds more like corporate bullshit. I wonder if any help has actually trickled down to Encino."

"Well, those miners must be needing rooms and food and transportation. That's gotta be good for the town, right?"

"I suppose, but my last email from Jack was about a month ago and he said things were pretty quiet. American had always owned a half a dozen houses at the north end of town along the ridge so maybe that's where the miners are living, assuming they're even there. Jack didn't seem to know much."

"Well, they still need to eat and drink and buy gas for their cars so something must be happening."

We drove a little farther and I said, "Hey, pull over up here by that Hackberry grove. If we stand on that hill we should be able to keep an eye on the drone while it's airborne."

We stopped and after Saul finished checking his camera and battery settings we looked at the map of the ranch that I'd picked up at the Capitol.

We decided to make a long sweep around the entire perimeter and then move in toward the remains of the old house and barn. We could only guess where the well was located. Saul planned to make a few low and slow search passes at the end of the run. Within ten minutes we were watching the drone do its work. I noticed a number of badly faded *No Trespassing* signs tacked to the old fence posts along the property line. I couldn't help but wonder if they'd been seen by the unknown person who'd discovered the Indian artifacts.

It took almost an hour to run the complete property line and get shots of the burned out barn and house. There were faint signs of vehicle activity but decades of overgrowth had obscured any hint of where the original horse trails and most of the burned corpse of the ranch house. The old corral fences had long ago collapsed but were slightly visible in the grass and scrub. The main entrance to the ranch was off of a narrow road at the end of the property opposite from where we stood. We'd decided that the well must be somewhere near the house along the entrance drive where it would have been easy to access. Saul flew that part of the route very slowly and then guided the drone back to a soft landing twenty feet from us. We'd have to examine the video very carefully back in Saul's studio to see if we'd found anything that looked like a well.

As we packed the drone back into the Jeep I looked down the road. "You know, that didn't take as long as I'd figured it would. How about we head on down another mile or two and stop in to see if Jack is around?"

Saul smiled and nodded. "Man, you just can't get Encino out of your head, can you?"

"Geez, aren't you the least bit curious about what's been going on there since our story went on the air?"

"Yeah, I guess maybe a little, but after we got started with Wade and everything that happened with him I sort of lost interest in Encino." He finished hooking the bungee cords over the drone and walked around to the driver's side. "Okay, I guess since we're so close we should at least stop and say hello. But we have bills to pay so let's keep our focus on this ranch."

I nodded in agreement, struck by how my once Bohemian friend had changed his focus. He almost sounded like a businessman.

A few minutes later we reached the intersection and turned into the gas station. We couldn't help but notice the changes. The weathered Texaco sign had been painted over with the message *Jack's Fuel Stop*. The old wood siding had also been freshly painted a bright yellow and a simple, flat roofed canopy had been built over the two pumps. It was clear that Jack had decided to stick around awhile. Saul pulled over to the side of the building. We'd no sooner stepped out onto the asphalt when a beaming Jack burst from the doorway. "Holy shit, look who's back!" he shouted.

We all traded smiles and handshakes and I said, "Believe it or not, Jack, we were in the neighborhood."

"Yeah, right. The only neighborhood around here is us and there's not much left of it."

Saul chimed in. "Well, there's the old, abandoned ranch up the road. We were checking it out for a possible story. There was some kind of Indian artifact heist on the place."

Jack nodded. "Yeah, I heard somethin' about that. Sounds like bullshit to me. The place has been empty since before I was born. We used to fly our kites in the empty pasture when we were kids."

"Were the No Trespassing signs posted back then?" I asked.

"Yeah, but did you ever know a kid who paid attention to signs?" He turned toward the door. "Come on in. I just made a fresh pot if you're interested."

Jack had cleaned up the inside of the station and there were new displays of motor oil, wiper blades and all the miscellaneous little things every car owner needs. We stood around the sales counter and caught each other up on things that had gone on in our lives. It felt good to see Jack again after all that had happened in his town. He seemed relaxed but when I asked him what was going on with the mine reopening his demeanor changed.

"Well, I guess that depends on who you ask." His smile had faded. "There's been a whole shit load of people runnin' around town but they're not real talkative. They come here for gas, stop at Rita's to eat and they get a good crowd for drinks at The Bond and once in a while someone even rents a room. But they're careful about sayin' too much. We were told we'd get regular updates from American but that hasn't happened. Anytime we want to know somethin' we have to ask someone in Denver and then wait for an answer. Sometimes that takes a whole week. They're bein' tight lipped about things. Russell and I had been takin' turns drivin' up to the mine to see things for ourselves but they blocked the damn road near the entrance last week so we can't see much now."

Somehow I wasn't surprised. "Before they blocked the road did you get a look at what's going on?

"Well, they're tryin' to put things back in order. The benches look pretty much like they did when things were rollin' along but that's it. Nothin' has changed. So far the crews haven't come back, just enough guys to kick up a little dust and make a little noise. And whatever they're doin' it doesn't involve the benches. The trucks and equipment are just sittin' there."

"What about improvements to the town itself, like infrastructure, anything going on there?"

"Not much. When the story first came out about the reopenin' they told us they were goin' to start with an inspection of the streets and the utilities. A month later we had to practically beg em' to see a copy of it.

"What'd it say?"

"There wasn't much to it. There was nothin' about the streets or overhead lines, just the stuff underground. All they wanted were the locations of the pipes and lines and all the buried shit. After they got that they passed it on to the County and the State to see who's gonna pay for any work that might be needed."

Saul shook his head. "That's kind of strange. So what about getting some businesses to come back?"

"That's the hardest part. It's like Catch 22. Do you open businesses so the people will move back or do you wait for the people and then open your doors? Meanwhile the god-damn banks are 'sitting on their hands waitin' to see who makes the first move. I'm just rollin' the dice with the improvements I've done."

"What about those houses that American owns up on the ridge?"

"Well, there's a bunch of their guys livin' in em' now but if and when they bring on a bigger crew there's gonna be a problem. There's still empty houses everywhere and somebody's gonna have to do some real work on most of em'. They're really run down. That means goin' to the banks and the people who still own em' to see who's willin' to pay for what."

"So how about Russell and Rita, what are they saying about it all?"

"They're like me, they'll believe it when they see it. Like I said, they're getting' a little more business from the guys who moved in but it ain't much. There's a meetin' with American scheduled here in town in a week or so and Russell already has a long list of shit to put in front of them. Rita is loaded for bear too. And there's a few more of us hangers-on that say they're gonna show up for it."

"Is there any kind of buzz going on, any kind of activity from the other folks who are still here?"

"Well, that's another strange thing. Joe Theobald and a couple other people got letters from a company in Denver. The letter said the company wanted to buy their properties and they'd pay cash. And they said they wanted a decision like right now."

That struck me as odd. "Why did they get the letter and not you and everyone else in town?"

"I have no idea. The only thing I could come up with was that all their houses and land are along the boundary between the town line and the mine."

Saul had been scrolling on his phone and interrupted. "Hey, guys, I've gotta' be getting back home soon but I thought we should make a quick trip up to the mine before we go. Jack, could my Jeep get around that roadblock?"

"Yeah, I think so. It's on level ground and it's just a couple of sawhorses and a sign tellin' you to turn around. Russell and I weren't feelin' too adventurous when we were there so that's what we did."

Saul's idea had taken me by surprise. "What are you thinking of?"

"Nothing big, maybe a few photos if we can get close enough."

"We came here for the ranch story, not to get our asses in trouble with the miners again. We already told that story."

Jack appeared puzzled. "Yeah, what the hell are you thinkin'?"

Saul nodded. "I'm not looking for trouble or anything like that. I'm just curious about what's going on and even more curious about what's not going on." He turned and looked at straight at me. "Keep in mind, partner, that if it hadn't been for us, those bastards would've gotten away with a fortune in silver and nobody would have ever heard of what's going on around here. That sign that says *Turn Around* should say *Welcome Saul and Jay.*"

He had a point. Our documentary about Encino had led to repercussions that no one had ever expected but it also exposed a major crime. The stockholders of American Mining surely lost some money. Our work on the documentary and what we'd discovered kept it from being a whole lot worse. Jack looked like he was waiting for me to say something. I just shrugged, looked at Saul and said, "Oh shit, I guess it wouldn't hurt to get a quick look at the place. But we'll stay up on the ridge, no closer. Maybe get a few pics but no drone. That's it. Deal?"

"Deal."

Jack walked us out to the Jeep. Just before we pulled away he held up his right hand and said, "If anyone up there gives you any shit you come right back here and tell me. I'll deal with it." Then he smiled.

It was clear that Jack had enjoyed his recent time back in his police uniform. "Thanks, man. We'll be in touch soon."

The drive down Railroad Street was the same eerily quiet trip it had always been. A car was parked in front of Rita's Café and a pickup truck another block down. There was no traffic. We couldn't see any sign of activity at The Bond. If there was anything happening on the possible revival of the town it didn't show. When we got to the turn on to Shit Street Saul said, "I expected to see more than that."

I nodded and sighed. "Still not dead, but almost."

The cloud of dust near the mine that we'd seen earlier was gone and when we reached the top of the ridge we saw the sign. It was just like Jack had described it; two sawhorses and a large cardboard sign with red letters reading TURN AROUND NOW. My guess was they hadn't put too much effort into a roadblock because they weren't expecting any visitors. Saul stopped in front of the barricade and asked, "So, partner, do we turn around or keep going?"

It only took me a few seconds to think about it. "Let's keep going, slow so we don't kick up a lot of dust. I want to see if there's anything happening down at the mine shack. That was where we saw the good stuff last time."

"Okay, but how about you drive and I'll grab a camera?" We switched places and I backed up and pulled around the sawhorses. We drove slowly down the rutted road toward the mine. It only took a minute to reach the pull-off area that we'd used before to take photos. I turned on to it and then faced the Jeep back down the road in case we had to make a quick exit. Saul stepped out and made sure he stayed behind the trees and rocks while he snapped photos. I grabbed a pair of binoculars and scanned the area below. There were two small trucks parked near the office shack but no sign of any miners. When I moved to scan the area at the base of the cliff I saw something that hadn't been there on our last little secret visit. "Hey, man, get a shot of those tanks. They weren't there last time we were snooping."

Saul nodded and started to pan the area with multiple shots. The large yellow tanks were labeled AMMONIUM CARBONATE. I had no idea what that was but I intended to find out. There was also a large truck with a drill boom mounted to the back end of it. Finally, when a man emerged from the office and headed for a pickup truck I said, "Okay, that's it for now. Let's get the hell out of here."

When I hit the gas pedal a little too hard Saul was thrown back against the seat. "Holy shit, man, take it easy. I almost lost my camera."

"Sorry, I just want to stay ahead of that guy. No sense drawing attention to ourselves like last time." We made it back to Railroad Street and I pulled over to the curb. We sat there waiting and a few minutes later the pickup truck passed us. The driver never looked in our direction. We got out and switched places again. As we headed back up Route 285 I looked out over the Roessler Ranch. It was the reason for our trip but once again Encino was on my mind.

Staying Focused

The drive back to Albuquerque seemed a bit longer than usual. It was probably because our conversation kept swinging back and forth between the ranch project and Encino. I could tell that despite working on the ranch mystery Saul was just as curious as I was about the unanswered questions that surrounded the revival of the town. With all we had to do on the Roessler video review it didn't seem that we should even be thinking about a previous project. We didn't have the luxury of a lot of time for both.

About half an hour outside of Albuquerque I got a text message from Katie. *"Lana and I are meeting for Happy Hour. Meet us at Gardunos if you get back in time."* I turned to Saul. "Any interest in meeting our women folk for a drink?"

"Yeah, I could use a beer." He paused then added, "They'll be curious about the ranch but how much do you want to tell them about Encino?"

It was a question I'd been asking myself ever since we'd started back. "Oh, let's just keep it to a quick stop to say hello to Jack, nothing else. At this point there's not much to say anyway."

Now that Lana had moved in with Saul, the four of us getting together for drinks had become a regular thing. We shared stories from our workdays, talked about current events and of course enjoyed our beverages of choice. We were at a table, half an hour into things before Katie asked the question I knew would be coming. "So, did you drive over to Encino while you were so close?"

I glanced over at Saul then back to Katie and nodded. "Yep, we stopped by the station to say hello to Jack and catch up."

Lana hadn't been around during the Encino project and wasn't clear on the names and places. "I saw the documentary but I don't remember all the names. Which one is Jack?"

Saul answered, "He runs the gas station and was sort of our point man whenever we were in town."

Katie added, "He's also the town cop. He was the one who arrested the crooked miners, the bad guys."

Lana turned back to Saul. "You mean like Carl and Bernie in Nashville? Are there bad guys on all of your projects?"

Saul and I looked at each other with the same eye rolling expression. Before either of us could answer Katie chimed in. "Lana, get used to it. These guys have a knack for finding trouble when they're working on something that looks normal to everyone else." I quickly jumped in and managed to steer the conversation in another direction. There was no more mention of bad guys.

Reviewing the drone video took up most of the next afternoon. The average person would see it as a boring view of huge, grassy fields and stands of scrub trees. The burned out wreckage of the structures was mostly grown over by weeds and brush and there was little sign of what had been the entrance road and driveway. The corrals were mostly toppled and covered with wild Blue Grama. The low altitude passes the drone had made revealed little else and we still couldn't determine the exact location of the well. We saw signs that a vehicle had recently been on the property and a large pile of cut brush sat near the vehicle tracks but nothing else. We'd have to make another visit and walk the site.

While Saul packed up his equipment I opened us a couple of beers. We sat on the patio to plan our strategy for the site visit and I had a feeling we were thinking the same thing. "Hey, man, I gotta ask. Have you been thinking about Encino as much as I have?"

He nodded and I waited for him to take a long pull on his beer. "Yeah, I have and I wish I could just get it out of my head."

"Doesn't it seem like there's something going on with American, something shady?"

"It feels that way to me. After we revealed the silver scam I thought for sure the Board and their management would go all out to make things right with the town. It sure looks like it's business as usual with them."

"And making cash offers on just the houses along the town limits is a big red flag. Why those houses? The whole town needs to be fixed." We sat silently for a while and then I said, "Okay, we have a project to focus on. Jack said he'd call me before the big meeting. Let's forget about Encino for now."

By the time we wrapped up our meeting we'd agreed to head back to the ranch as soon as we heard back from the granddaughter. That would give me time for more research on the history and Saul time for more photo review. My first task had to be contacting the woman for permission to be on the property. That would mean I'd have to tell her about the documentary which would have to include talk about the Indian artifacts. There was every chance she would deny us permission. I had to come up with an enticing sales pitch for why she should give us the okay. I had no idea what to say yet and she could make or break the project with her response. A turn down would end things right then and there. Permission would allow us to finish our concept pitch to *Disney+* or *Netflix*. It all had to happen soon if we had any hope of getting some seed money.

It felt almost primitive to be writing a letter and using snail mail to deliver it but since a post office box was the only contact information I had that's all I could do. From my digging at the capitol I'd found the name of Lynette Anne Roessler Harmon and the P.O. box number. A Google search didn't turn up much else. A carefully worded message on our new letterhead was the only way to reach out to her. I decided not to mention our Encino documentary in my letter. Ever since our visit with Jack I'd had a funny feeling about what was going on with the mine. The ranch was uncomfortably close to a whole lot of unanswered questions and it seemed prudent to keep the two topics separate. It was probably unfounded paranoia but time would tell.

Meanwhile

"Okay, I've read this report three times and I still don't know what the hell it says. How about one of you engineering eggheads tells me what I'm looking at. Stan, talk to me."

"Mike, it's like I told you before you left for vacation. This is a very preliminary report on what we found after our first try with the ISR method. In-situ Recovery isn't the digging and scraping you're used to in conventional mining so a lot of what's in the report is just chemistry. And I can tell you that the ammonium carbonate we injected in our first few tests has already shown very positive results."

"I'm not a god damned chemist, Stan, bottom line it for me."

"Okay, based on these early test injections we've recovered some copper, the silver we figured was down there with it and also gold in a concentrations that look very promising."

"And tell me again why you're so hot for this in-situ method. I've heard of it used for uranium mining but that's all. It doesn't sound like the copper mining I know."

"That's because it isn't. In-situ recovery allows us to extract the minerals without disrupting the surface of the land. There's no fracking involved and there's minimal environmental impact to the surface of the land. We inject the ammonium carbonate under pressure and when we pull it back out we can separate the minerals from the solution. The geology of this part of the country is perfect for it."

"I like the sounds of that. Why didn't American start doing this sooner and just shut down the pit? Nobody ever told me anything about this."

"The technology is fairly new and the pit was a steady, reliable operation. We wanted to do a test run before we brought you in."

"Last time I checked I'm way above your pay grade so who is the "we" that wanted to keep me in the dark?"

"Sorry, Mike, I can't say anything more for now. We didn't want any rumors spreading about a copper operation that's turning up silver and gold. People would be hounding you and the entire front office for answers."

"Well, your silent treatment pisses me off but I'll accept it for now. I agree if you're talking about silver and gold we'd better keep that quiet. We've already got a black eye for being a copper company that wasn't watching while their guys were stealing silver. News like this won't exactly help polish our corporate image. It isn't good for our stock either. And we sure as hell don't want to start a goddamned gold rush."

"Mike, there's something else you should know and I might as well tell you now."

"Oh great. I'm the guy in charge of southwest operations and you came all the way from Chicago to tell me what's going on in my backyard. So what the hell is it?"

"Well, it has to do with the land, the land all around the mine, including Encino. The thing with using in-situ is that you can't control exactly where the chemical injections will go once they're in the ore field. The injection well blows it in into the ground under very high pressure and we have to drill a grid of extraction wells around it. The problem is we can't always be sure we're extracting everything we injected."

"What happens if you don't get it all back out?"

"Well, usually nothing. In wide open land some of the chemical just stays in the ground."

"I smell trouble. Here we have the little town of Encino at our front door. What do we do when there's some nasty chemical in the ground and there are people nearby?"

"Let's just say we're working on that problem. We have a financial group, Todd Capital, that will probably become our partner if things work out. They're making offers to some of the remaining residents so we can acquire their property and eliminate any question marks."

What do you mean by question marks?"

Well, some of the properties are tied to the city water main but a lot of them have their own wells. And the main aquifer for the town has never been mapped properly. We can't risk getting the chemicals into the only water supply that some of those people have."

"Jesus, that's just great."

"Yeah, it's a real problem. The ground is a lot more valuable than the shitty little town sitting on it. That's why we have to buy out and get rid of anyone who's still living there. It's as simple as that."

"The hell it is. Look, Stan, we already got a big black eye for cutting all those jobs and emptying out the town. We're still feeling the backlash from the media. They want to know when the mine's going to reopen and when the jobs are coming back like we promised. It's just a matter of time before the TV crews show up again and they'll be expecting to see a shitload of miners and townspeople."

"We've already thought of that. We're bringing in some old crushers and haul trucks from Carlota and we even got hold of an old conveyor belt from Silver Bell. In a few days it'll look like a working mine again, at least from a distance."

"So, no men, just rusty old equipment."

"Yeah, that's the idea. As far as the recommissioning is concerned we're just treading water. We're just stalling for time until we can take ownership of the town, at least the properties that we'll need access to. We can make it look like we're the good guys helping out the locals and saving the environment."

"There's a Board of Director's meeting on the fifteenth of next month. They're going to want to hear all the warm and fuzzy things that are going on. I already got a draft agenda and the Encino status is on it. We're going to need to come up with convincing photos and a good story to tell."

"I saw the agenda too and we're already working on some things for you to present."

"There you go with that damn "we" thing again. Who the hell are you talking about?"

"All in due time, Mike, all in due time."

"Well god-dammit I don't want to look like an idiot, so you and I are going to have to be joined at the hip until then. I want to know every god damned thing that happens so I don't get blind-sided by some yokel reporter."

"Mike, I understand. Don't worry. These are simple folks and I'm sure we can handle them."

Sometimes You Get Lucky

When a phone number with a 310 area code appeared on my screen my first thought was "I don't know anyone there". It wasn't familiar and I figured I'd just let it go to voicemail. A minute later the voicemail chime sounded and I pulled the car over to answer it. I don't like to use the phone while I drive but the message made me wish I'd answered. It simply said, "Mr. Rorbach this is Lynette Harmon. I got your note in today's mail and I think we should talk. Please call me at this number." It was brief and to the point. I'd been mentally rehearsing a conversation with her but as I sat there I was suddenly at a loss for words.

After a few more moments of thought I punched in her number. It rang twice and I heard, "Hello, Mr. Rorbach."

"Hello, Lynette, may I call you Lynette? Thanks for getting back to me so quickly, and please call me Jay."

"Well, Jay, from what you said in your note it sounded kind of urgent. But I have to start by saying I'm not exactly sure how you think I can help you."

"To be honest I'm not sure either. Like I said in my letter I'm working on a storyline for a documentary that involves your property, the old ranch. I just thought I should reach out to let you know and to get your permission to look around the place."

There was a brief silence and then, "Jay, I haven't set foot on that ranch since I was twelve years old. I'm not sure why my parents hung on to it but my grandfather insisted that it stay in the family. If it were up to me I'd sell it but my son thinks otherwise."

"Back in the day it was a beautiful working ranch. I've seen a few old photographs."

"My son, Tom, says the same thing but that was a long time ago. I have to keep reminding him he's a lawyer not a cowboy."

I laughed. "Oh, I think there's a little bit of cowboy in most guys, they just don't get a chance to let it out."

We talked for a while and I told her a few of the things I'd learned about her grandfather and the early days of the ranch. I gave her a very abbreviated description of the artifacts side of the story. I also told her about the documentary we'd done on the mine and Encino and its proximity to the ranch. She seemed only mildly interested and when I was finished all she said was, "Okay, so you want my permission to go on to the ranch so you can do your story."

"Right. It should probably be in writing or even just an email so it's on record."

"Like I said I really don't care much about the place but my son does so how about I have him send you something, like maybe a permission letter. He'll know what it should say.'

"Sounds perfect. We'd like to do it soon so I hope he can jump on it."

"Don't worry,' she said with a laugh, "Tom still listens to his mother."

By the following afternoon I'd taken my research as far as I could. We were dead in the water until we could do the walking tour of the property. I knew if things dragged on too long Saul would start in on me with something like, "Maybe that golfer story isn't so bad after all." The longer the delay the longer moving the story along the longer we'd have to wait for any chance of income. I considered it an omen when I checked my email and saw a message from Attorney Thomas Harmon. It was probably the shortest message an attorney ever sent: *Mr. Rorbach, please call me at the number below.*"

I called him back immediately not having any idea what to expect. After a five minute hold he finally got on the phone. "Sorry for the long wait, Mr. Rorbach, it's one of those days around here."

"No problem, and please call me Jay."

"Okay, and I'm Tom. My mother filled me in on your conversation and what happened at the ranch. Anything new on that front?"

I liked his "get to the point" approach. "Well, no, as far as we know. My partner and I took some drone photos and video just to establish a baseline for the status of the property. I'll send you copies of everything."

"That'd be great. I haven't seen the place since my uncle took me there when I was a kid. I've been wanting an excuse to go back and this just might be it. I see that you're based in Albuquerque so I can fly into there and we can drive to the ranch together. Would that work for you?"

"Sounds perfect, when do you want to do it?"

"I'll have the case I'm working on wrapped up by the end of the week. How about I get a Monday flight?"

"That'd be great. I appreciate your willingness to get involved so quickly. My partner and I want to keep things cranking on the story."

"Well, Jay, the story means a lot to me too. It's a family story I've thought about my whole life and how it feels like some kind of mystery."

"And now here's your chance to start unraveling it."

There's Something
Going On

Katie and I were looking forward to some down time and a quiet weekend. When I saw Jack's number appear on my phone screen on Saturday morning I wondered if our quiet time was about to get louder. The fact he was calling me instead of sending an email was telling. I let it go to voicemail and then walked out to the patio to make the call, out of earshot of Katie.

It rang only once before I heard, "Mornin' Jay. Hey thanks for callin' back so fast. I have some news, big news, at least I think so."

"Good news or bad news?"

"Hard to say. I got a registered letter yesterday from American. They want to bring a bunch of people here to meet with us, as many of us as we can gather. They're callin' it an update on what's goin' on at the mine."

"That sounds pretty normal. When I was in Encino you told me it was going to happen pretty soon."

"Yeah, I did but there's more. They're bringin' along a couple of people who want to talk about buyin' up some properties. It was kind of vague but they want to see as many of us we can round up. The letter included an attachment with a list of properties that are empty. It includes houses and businesses. Jay, they even want to buy the school and the Catholic church. They wanna' buy a fuckin' church. What do you make of all that?"

It took me a few seconds to collect my thoughts. "Uh, I'm not sure. Something doesn't smell right. First they said they'd reopen the mine to save the town and now they want to buy it instead. It makes no sense."

"That's what I thought too. I showed the letter to Russell and he's as confused as I am. He's already started callin' people to show up. He said we'll set the date for it after he hears back from everybody. The letter said they want to meet by the end of this month because they have some big meetin' of their own on the fifteenth of next month."

The patio door slid open and Katie stepped out. She nodded toward the phone.

"It's Jack from Encino. He has some news about a meeting with the mining people.'

Her expression wasn't unexpected. She wanted a laid back weekend by ourselves and her face told me the call wasn't on her agenda. I nodded and went back to the conversation. "Hey, Jack, I have to run. Can we talk again, maybe on Monday?"

Jack seemed caught off guard but answered, "Ah, sure thing but we really need to talk about this so call me for sure."

"Will do. See ya'."

Before I could explain anything Katie said, "You didn't have to cut your call short, I was just surprised it was Jack calling you on a weekend."

"That's okay, it can wait until Monday. He just wanted to tell me about a meeting with the mining company that's coming up."

Her long sigh said a lot and she added, "All that time you spent on the documentary and all the media coverage and nothing's changed." She sat down across the table from me. "Honey, I know you're a part of the story as much as those people are but can't we just have a nice weekend, the two of us without anyone from Encino?"

I knew she was right and that we were long overdue for a "couple's weekend". With an upcoming Monday meeting with Tom Harmon and a visit to the ranch, thoughts of Encino would be pushed into the background. And both topics would have to take a backseat to Katie for the next two days. It was going to be an effort but I owed it to her. We were heading to Santa Fe and Katie and I knew a lot of ways to tune out everything but each other.

Digging In

Tom Harmon's plane was on time and after hurried introductory handshakes at the terminal entrance Tom, Saul and I headed toward the ranch. Tom's enthusiasm for the trip was obvious. The drive across I-40 gave him good views of the high desert and the mountains, views I'd seen my whole life but never tired of. Our conversation about the ranch and the artifacts mystery was constantly interrupted by his comments about the impossibly blue sky, the magenta hills and the native vegetation. I had a feeling that Saul was as amused as I was with Tom's Western attire. I was pretty sure his shiny cowboy boots were newly purchased for this trek to the ranch. And I couldn't help but wonder if at some point he was going to pull a Stetson out of his luggage

Saul shared the drone photos with him and pointed out the remnants of the structures. Despite the fact he was looking at burned out ruins Tom seemed excited and even referred to the place as "My ranch".

We merged onto Route 285 and about fifteen minutes later I said, "Okay, Tom, look to your right. There it is, that's your ranch."

He was silent for a moment and I noticed a faint smile as he gazed over the grassy fields. "So beautiful" was all he said.

We pulled on to the small graveled utility road that led to the ranch entrance. The dust and rough surface made me regret volunteering to drive. The gap between two sections of broken down fence seemed like a good place to turn in and park. While Saul opened the rear hatch to pull out his video camera I stood beside the car and watched as Tom slowly walked around, silently taking in the views of what was once his great grandfather's home. Seeing up close the ruins of the house and barn and thinking of the old photos I'd seen of them in their heyday was like looking at ghosts.

Saul and I went about our business and gave Tom some distance. He walked around the burned out house while he glanced at copies of the old photographs I'd collected. We figured his thoughts were on his great-grandfather and the Old West elegance that had died there. The faint smile we'd seen before never left his face. The urban cowboy was enjoying himself.

"Let's give him some time alone" I said quietly to Saul. We walked toward the spot where we thought the old well was located and found an opening in the years of weeds and brush that surrounded it. It was clear that someone had recently cut back the vegetation. The well was a circular stone wall about five feet in diameter and three feet high. We leaned over the edge and peered into the darkness below. There was nothing but dust and the remnants of an old rope hanging from a rusted iron hook.

I looked around at the brush and scrub grass. "Whoever found this well must have had a clue it was here because they would have had to chop their way through all that creosote and ironwood to even get a glimpse of it."

Saul nodded. "Yeah, as though they'd been here before." He had a still camera around his neck while he held a video camera and panned the area around the well.

I walked away so I wouldn't block his shots. About thirty yards from the well I came upon a large pile of branches and cuttings. As I stepped around it I noticed a yellow pipe near the edge of the pile. I thought to myself that whatever it was it looked like it didn't belong there. When I kicked some of the branches aside and bent down for a closer look I knew I was right. The pipe was part of an assembly of pipes, valves and what looked like a pump, not exactly what you'd expect to find on an old cattle ranch. It appeared that a larger, vertical pipe had been removed from the assembly and was lying on the ground beside it. A small metal tag, almost like a military dog-tag, hung from the handle on a valve. I wiped the dust from it and felt a chill when I read the words: PROPERTY OF AMERICAN MINING & EXTRACTION. I turned back toward Saul. "Holy shit, man, you gotta see this!"

He walked over and bent down for a closer look while I kicked more of the branches away. He read the tag and looked up at me. "Why in hell would American be messing around on this piece of land? It's not their property."

"I wondered the same thing. And what's with all the pipes? That doesn't look like mining to me."

Saul stood up and after I cleared more debris away he took photos of the equipment. He'd no sooner finished when Tom joined us. He looked at the pipes and asked, "What's all this?"

"We don't have a clue. There's a tag that says it belongs to American Mining, the guys that run the strip mine up the road."

"This is my family's land and I'm in charge of the estate. I know for a fact we never gave anyone permission to do any mining here."

My head was filled with thoughts of Jack's story about the mysterious offers to buy certain properties in Encino. I wondered if the pipes and activity on the Roessler ranch were somehow connected to those offers. "Well, Tom, we thought your visit was going to be pretty simple but I think this sort of complicates things."

"What do you mean?"

"I mean it looks like there's stuff going on around here, stuff that doesn't make sense and I have a feeling it's all somehow tied to the activity in Encino."

Saul nodded. "I agree. As soon as I saw that tag with American Mining's name on it I knew something didn't smell right."

Tom looked back and forth at us then said, "Guys, I'm kind of the new kid on the block. How about filling me in on what's going on here. What doesn't smell right?" He seemed rattled.

Saul looked at me. "Jay, you fill him in. You're the one who's been doing the legwork on this."

"Okay." I pointed toward the east. "Tom, over that hill about a mile and a half from here is the town of Encino. It used to be a pretty nice place when the copper mine was in full production. The mine belongs to American Mining. A couple of years ago, with no notice to the miners, they slowed down the operation and people lost their jobs. The slowdown became pretty much a shutdown and Encino shut down with it. Most of the people left. American never said anything official about closing the mine and kept everyone in the dark. The handful of ranchers and townspeople who stayed kept hoping things would get back to normal eventually."

"I take it that didn't happen."

"No it didn't. It's a long story and Saul and I made a documentary to tell it. I'll send you a link so you can watch it. But what it all came down to was that American Mining wasn't paying attention to what was going on. They have a big portfolio of mining operations in the United States and Canada and Encino was one of the small ones."

"So why did they shut it down?"

""They claim that they never did, at least officially. It seems a small number of executives, with the help of some less than honest miners, found a big vein of silver away from the main copper pit. They cooked up a scheme to keep the find from going public and they didn't even tell their Board. They shifted the operation to extracting the silver and selling it over the border to avoid any scrutiny.

"So Encino was dying and American just let it happen?"

"Yep, that's pretty much it. And a lot of good people suffered."

Saul chimed in, "After our documentary told the story, American was shamed into fixing things, recommissioning the mine and bringing the town back to life. They made a big deal of going on television and making promises. From what we've heard and seen since then it was all bullshit."

Tom looked confused and didn't respond for a few seconds. Finally he said, "Okay, that's a sad story and I feel bad for those people but I'm not seeing how that ties into these pipes on my land."

"We don't either," I answered, "but you've gotta believe that if American is involved it's not in the best interests of the people around here including you."

Tom was clearly upset. "Well, at the risk of sounding like a lawyer this all looks like criminal trespass and willful damage to private property. This is my land and there's no way in hell I'm gonna put up with this bullshit."

"I don't blame you," Saul said. "Those corporate bastards have been running roughshod around here and maybe this is a chance to stop it, or at least find out what they're up to."

The lawyer in Tom came out even stronger. "Okay, these people trespassed on my land. There's clear evidence of some form of drilling activity by a company whose business is the removal of something from the ground...my ground. That's theft." He stepped back and looked around at the pipes and the vehicle tracks. "Saul, if you don't mind, can I ask you to take some photos of all of this? I'm going to need some evidence of what they've been doing."

"Glad to. I'd love to nail these bastards. I mean in a legal way."

Tom helped me move the limbs and brush away from the pipes and about ten minutes later Saul had a clear, wide view of the immediate area. He took shots from several vantage points, panned the parts of the field with the vehicle tracks and even got a close-up shot of the metal tag. I kept looking at Tom as he watched Saul working. The faint smile had returned to his face. The lawyer was enjoying himself.

The three of us spent another hour walking the ranch from fence to fence and comparing the place to the old photographs. It was easy to see why James Roessler had chosen it. The gently rolling pasture land and the incredible views of the surrounding hills were like something straight out of Hollywood. It made me wonder if, had he lived longer, Roessler would have filmed a Western there. We watched as Tom, his great-grandson scanned the views around him. Despite his concerns over the mysterious pipes, his smile had returned.

The conversation on the drive back to Albuquerque bounced around from the ranch to the well, the pipes and the upcoming meeting in Encino. We agreed that the pipes were a huge red flag that something was going on, something American Mining was being secretive about. They were the big dog and the few remaining people in Encino could get bitten. We agreed that the bigger the turnout the better and Tom said he'd consider flying back to join us. And I had an idea for one more very special guest; my old miner friend Billy Pickett.

Okay, here's the plan

"Stan, come on in, have a seat. I was just getting ready to call you."

"I'm glad I caught you, Mike. I'm heading to the airport in a few minutes and I have the agenda here for your meeting in Encino. It's just these three pages. I wanted to run it by you so you'll be ready to field any questions from the local yokels."

"Aren't you going to be there too?"

"No, we decided it's best if we don't send a lot of our people. We don't want to make it look like it's too big a deal, you know, and make them suspicious. It'll just be you, Isaac and Charlotte."

"Charlotte? Why do we need her?"

"Well, she put together most of the files so she knows the history. And having a woman in the mix gives us a friendlier look. I already told her not to say too much, just kind of be there and smile at the folks. This whole dog and pony show will be in your hands."

"This looks pretty simple, Stan, not a lot of details about the In-situ drilling. That's good, the less they know about that shit the better."

"Yeah, we concentrated on the whole save the environment thing, the Clean Air Act and shit like that. We figure that'll be enough to stop a lot of their questions. Mostly you'll be making it seem like we're looking out for their best interests and willing to help them leave with some money in their pockets."

"And what if someone doesn't want to leave? I can't believe how some of them have hung on this long."

"Mike, relax, those people have got to be just about out of money and hope. I'm betting we can buy them out for next to nothing. Look over the numbers on Page three. Charlotte put together that spread sheet and those are the offers that Todd Capital came up with."

"I'm no real estate expert but they don't exactly look generous."

"They're not but we look at it like it's a buyer's market. The people who still live there are broke or damn close to it. They know there isn't a long line of people waiting to buy their places. Those folks don't want to come to grips with the fact their lousy little town is dead. And you gotta believe the banks that are still holding the paper on the empty places will grab the first damned offer we give them."

"Wait a minute, Stan, something's missing here. What about all of the public relations bullshit that American's been spewing, the promises about reopening the pit and bringing back the jobs? That's what they're expecting to hear next week. They know there's a huge demand for copper. Christ, it's in every battery and cellphone in the world. Those people are going to be focused on the pit."

"Well, Mike, that's the challenge, your challenge. The new message is that American Mining wants to be a good steward of the land. The new extraction technology we'll be using is better for the environment. It's the future of mining and we're excited to be a part of it."

"Oh come on, Stan, do you really think these people are going to give a shit about the environment? They're desperate, they're barely hanging on."

"So that's when you turn to Page Three. That's when you announce our Fund the Future Plan."

"I gave that a quick scan. It looks like a bunch of parcel numbers and a dollar amount for each one. There's nothing about who came up with the values or how they arrived at them. Somebody in that crowd is going to ask about that. I know I would if it was my property."

"Okay, so maybe we'll have to ask Charlotte to get involved after all. She can talk about how Todd Capital was hired to figure the buyout part. I'll give her the talking points and make sure she sticks to them. The numbers will sound better coming from a woman. Or maybe we'll get someone from Todd to be there to answer questions. I'll get John Quinn to join you."

"Stan, you seem to think the people of Encino will be pushovers but I think you're wrong."

"Relax, Mike, it's like I said before, these are simple folks and I know we can handle them."

Laying the Groundwork

A hurried trip to Encino to meet with Jack and Russell and a whole lot of phone calls and emails later, our strategy for the meeting with American had taken shape. With help from the Torrance County School District we got access to the school building. It was the only place in town that could accommodate what we'd hoped would be a big crowd. The school district wanted to find out what might happen to their property and planned to send their lawyer and Superintendent. The County was sending a Commissioner and an Engineer. The Catholic Diocese was sending the former priest from the church. Two Santa Fe banks were planning to have representatives there to field information on some of the vacant houses and downtown buildings. Jack had rounded up a bunch of the locals to fill some seats. He'd even found a few people who'd left and were coming back to town to find out if they had a reason to return. When the gavel came down to open the meeting I had a feeling that American Mining was going to have its hands full.

I was on the fence about whether to attend until a phone call from Tom Harmon changed that. His anger over the trespassing and drilling on his ranch had only grown since his meeting with Saul and me. He had already made his flight and rental car arrangements. I knew that our hoped-for project about the ranch mystery was too important for us not to share the meeting with him.

Our tour of the ranch and the discovery of the yellow pipes had become an obsession with me. I had reached out to Billy Pickett to see, once again, if he could help me make sense of what we'd found. He'd been planning a trip back to Albuquerque to visit family and when I told him my story of the pipes and the big meeting with American I swear I could feel his smile over the phone. He agreed to schedule his visit around the American meeting. Saul emailed him some of the photos from our tour of the ranch and his reply was, "Wow, this is going to be an interesting little meeting."

It wasn't just our desire for a big turnout that gave me the idea. Ever since I'd first visited Encino and seen the places my father had enjoyed so much I'd wanted Katie to see it all too. Saul had told me several times that Lana asked a lot of questions about the place and wondered why it was so important to him. Since both women had fairly flexible schedules we talked them into taking their first trip to experience it first-hand. Russell had recently upgraded a few rooms at The Bond so I made the reservations. I knew that this trip to Encino was going to be unlike any of the ones I'd made before.

To Die or Not to Die

Saul, Katie, Lana and I purposely arrived in Encino two hours early for the meeting. A long, slow driving tour of the town was in order so the women could get a sense of what the place was now and what it used to be. As they looked around the sadness in their conversation was clear. Lana even talked about how the story of Encino could make a great Country song. Katie wondered how anyone could still be living there. The silence and emptiness at the center of the business district seemed almost eerie. When we got to the end of Railroad Street I said I was going to turn around but Saul had another idea. "Come on, man, we've come all this way and they really should see the mine. It's what everyone will be talking about tonight."

I reluctantly turned on to Shit Street and we began the slow ascent toward the mine. Katie and Lana said nothing as they looked out over the dusty, rolling hills. We were expecting to see the roadblock ahead but it was gone. We figured it must have been taken away to avoid any questions from curious meeting attendees who might be checking it out. We reached the crest of the hill and were surprised to see a man standing by a car at the edge of the road. My surprise faded when I saw it was Billy Pickett.

I pulled over and we all got out. While Saul gave the women a quick overview of the mine I walked over to Billy. "Well, I figured if anyone from the meeting would drive up here it'd be you."

"Hey, good to see you, Jay. Yeah, I just wanted to see the status of things, you know, how much activity."

"And what do you think? Is it what you expected?

He hesitated and shook his head. "Not in the least. I wondered why there was no dust in the air. Hell, a copper mine is a god-damned dust factory. And the demand for copper in our new Green Economy means this pit should be humming." He pointed toward the benches. "See that equipment? It's not being used. The way it's sitting there looks like it's just parked, like for show."

"So the mine's shut down?"

"Well, no, it isn't. The pit isn't active but there's some other shit going on over there by the tunnel entrance, by those tanks. They tell me a whole lot of what's going on around here."

"I wondered about them too, the other day when Saul and I were looking around. What are they for?"

"They're full of ammonium carbonate. It's used in the leaching process to separate the ore from the surrounding soil." He paused a moment then said, "Jay, it looks like American has switched to what's called in situ mining."

"What in the hell is that?"

"It's fairly new technology. I saw it being used in Nevada and Utah for uranium mostly but this is the first I've heard of it here in New Mexico. What they do is inject a leaching chemical into the ground, in this case the ammonium carbonate, It separates the ore from everything around it. Then they pump that liquid out of the ground and the ore comes with it. It's really kind of slick because they can get the ore without digging for it."

"So why wouldn't American be up front with everything and tell the people what they're doing? And what's with the digging equipment just sitting unused on the benches?"

"I have a hunch but I need to call a couple of guys about it. Let's head back to the hotel and maybe I can make some sense of all this before the meeting."

An hour later we were all gathered at the bar at The Bond. Russell was enjoying being host to the first crowd he'd had in his place in a very long time. Saul and I introduced Katie and Lana to our local friends and circulated through the growing group. Billy Pickett was sitting at the bar, taking on his phone and writing on note cards. I was as excited as I was apprehensive about what we were in for. A half hour into the gathering Katie took me aside and asked, "Is it me or is there something about to happen? I'm hearing a lot of chatter about confronting the people from American and I thought it was just supposed to be some kind of friendly update thing." Lana was standing nearby and added, "I was wondering the same thing. I heard a guy say he'd had enough shit from those people."

I understood their surprise because the people and situation were new to them. Our documentary had exposed the things that can happen when a corporation forgets about its responsibility to people but Katie and Lana were hearing it first hand in the place where it had been happening. It felt a lot more personal.

Not surprisingly the meeting got off to a late start. The school district had worked out a deal to get the heat and power turned back on. The air in the room was musty from having been closed up for nearly two years. Our group had to help place their own chairs in rows while the American Mining people stood behind two long tables at the front of the room. Encino residents were clustered in the front two rows. Off to the side of the room Jack stood ramrod straight in his Police Chief garb including his sidearm. Everyone in the room knew he was there and why. Next to him was Linda Ruiz, a KOB reporter and Scott, her cameraman. They had covered the raid on the mine when the silver theft was revealed and Jack had invited them back to cover the meeting. When things seemed to be in place everyone took a seat.

A tall, portly man with a graying beard that matched his suit stood up and waited for the room to quiet down. He held a microphone and finally said, "Ladies and gentlemen, welcome to this special meeting. I'm Michael Marshall. I'm Director of Southwest Operations for American Mining and I appreciate you all being here this evening. We have some exciting news for you and I think you're going to leave this meeting with smiles on your faces." He waited for a response from the audience but when I looked around I didn't see anyone smiling.

Marshall introduced the rest of his team: John Quinn from Todd Capital, Isaac Linzer, a Field Engineer from American and Charlotte Bestwick, whose title of Project Assistant was nebulous at best. She pressed a key on a laptop in front of her and a large map of the mine, Encino and the surrounding area appeared on a pull-down screen behind them. Marshall waited a moment for the crowd to look over the map and then began his spiel.

"As you can see this is a map, a current one, of our mining operation. It also shows the Town of Encino, the ranch country around it and the major highways." He waited a moment then continued. "If you're wondering what all of the little dotted lines are, those are the individual properties within the town limits. They show your homes and businesses and even the school we're sitting in right now." He paused again. The locals were whispering and pointing as they each located their spot on the map. "What we'd like to talk with you about tonight is what that map might look like in the future. He clicked the small remote control in his hand and a new map appeared. The whispers from the crowd turned into murmurs and then louder into outright anger. The map showed the dotted lines removed and the entire area labeled *American Mining*.

I looked over at Tom Harmon who was staring at the screen and shaking his head. The boundary lines for his ranch had been erased along with the other properties. Knowing he had to get control of the crowd Marshall held up his hands and said, "Okay, I'm sure this raises a lot of questions so if you'll quiet down I'm sure you'll like what I have to say."

A man whom I didn't recognize called out, "What are you guys gonna do, take over the whole damn town?"

Marshall looked rattled. Katie leaned over and said, "See, it's like I heard back at the hotel. These people are pissed already and it's just getting started."

"Well, I didn't think it was going to be a picnic. Hang on for the ride."

Marshall offered a weak smile and finally answered the man who'd shouted. "No, sir, we are not here to take over the town. Please, all of you, give my team a few minutes to fill you in on what we have in mind. First, let's hear from Isaac Linzer. He's been doing some engineering work I think you'll find interesting. Marshall handed Linzer the remote as they exchanged nervous looks. The crowd noise finally dwindled enough for Linzer to begin. The screen switched to a photo of a large tract of land filled with arrays of large pipes protruding from the ground surrounded by clusters of smaller pipes. "What you're looking at is, in my opinion, the future of mining. This is a mine in Nevada and we're using a new method of reaching the ore. It's called In-situ Recovery." He paused a few seconds then continued. "As you can see there is no digging, no dust from heavy equipment and no disruption to the wildlife. It's a new environmentally safe way to get the ore from the ground."

The same man who'd shouted before shouted again, "What are all those damn pipes for?" There are some like that stickin' out of the ground in Sarah Wheeler's yard next to my property and in two other yards down the street." Tom Harmon was staring intently at Marshall, waiting for the answer.

Billy Pickett was sitting on the other side of Katie. He leaned forward, turned to me and said, "Oh, Jesus, here we go."

It was clear that Linzer was a field guy and not used to public speaking. He spoke slowly and explained the process of injecting the leeching chemical, extracting the ore solution and separating the materials. Under ordinary circumstances it would have been a dry and boring topic but with people's homes and businesses on the line the crowd seemed transfixed. Marshall sat quietly with a fake looking smile stuck on his face as Linzer went on and on about American being proud stewards of the land. I looked over and saw Billy shuffling his note cards. When Linzer stopped and asked if anyone had questions Billy jumped up, waving his hand and shouting, "Yeah, over here. I got a few!"

I leaned toward Katie and said, "It's show time."

Billy cleared his throat and looked one by one at the four people at the front table. "My name is William Pickett. I'm a miner with thirty-six years of experience in copper, uranium and silver. Part of my time was underground and part was out in the pit." He glanced down at his notes then asked, "Would you please tell this group exactly what you are mining for with the in situ method?"

Linzer's face went blank. He turned toward Marshall as if he was looking for help. Marshall looked surprised as he stood up and looked at Billy. "Uh, well, I'm not sure I understand your question, sir. We've been mining copper here in Encino for a long time."

Billy nodded. "Sure, we all know the history of this mine. But I've never heard of in situ being used for copper. From what I've been told the ore and soil structure with copper is a dig-only situation. The ore is more widely dispersed through the base soil. In situ is supposed to be for metals that are found in more concentrated veins."

Marshall was clearly surprised and rattled. Saul looked over at me with a smirk and I wondered if he was thinking the same thing I was. It was obvious that Marshall hadn't expected a question from someone with Billy's knowledge. After an uncomfortable pause Marshall answered, "How about we hold the rest of the questions until we finish our presentation? We have more to share with you. Charlotte, let's pass out our report and let everyone look it over."

Charlotte moved down the rows of chairs handing each person the three page presentation that American hoped would get them through the meeting. Katie said softly, "They're stalling for time and it looks like Billy's pissed." I looked over and saw the scowl on his face as Charlotte handed him his copy. If Marshall really thought the hand-out would help him regain control of the meeting he got his answer just a moment later when Tom Harmon stood up and shouted, "You never answered that man's question about the pipes. There are pipes like those, your pipes, sticking out of the ground on my ranch and I never gave you permission to drill there. That's trespassing and I've got some other things I can charge you with."

I noticed that the KOB crew had moved forward, panning the room with their video camera. They turned their attention to the American representatives when the crowd noise began to grow. I could barely understand Marshall when he shouted, "Please everyone, let's all quiet down and look at page three of your handouts. That's what we need you to focus on!" He turned and nodded to a nervous looking John Quinn. The two men talked and it looked like Quinn wasn't buying whatever Marshall was saying. When Quinn started shaking his head back and forth an angry looking Marshall stepped forward, held up his handful of paperwork and called out, "Ladies and gentlemen, please turn to page three. We have money for you!"

There's nothing like the promise of money to get people's attention. Even I turned to page three. It only took a few seconds for the crowd to understand what they were looking at. American Mining wanted to buy Encino and everything around it. A man in the back row stood up and looked at Marshall. "I'm Anthony DeSantis. I'm Deputy General Manager for New Mexico Bank and Trust. We hold the deeds for a number of properties, residential and commercial, here in the Encino area. We have watched as our customers lost their homes when you slowed down your operations. We have watched as our commercial customers lost their businesses while you continued some amount of mining. My bank would like to get out from under these debts and we were hoping that American would be announcing new hiring to bring the people back. From what we've seen so far this evening that isn't your plan."

Marshall struggled to make a sincere smile. "Mr. DeSantis, I certainly understand your concern for the bank's position in all of this. Our proposal, what you see in our report, is that American Mining will purchase the properties shown on the map, at a fair market price. That's what we've shown on page three."

Father Gerhardt from Saint Mark's parish stood and interrupted. "Excuse me, but I'm looking at your so-called report and the price you have set for buying our church. I'm no real estate expert but even I can see you're low-balling us." Rita was sitting next to him and called out something that was drowned out by the crowd.

Tom Harmon took his turn. "I live in Los Angeles and I inherited my ranch. It's not in good shape right now but it can be and I'll tell you right now that I have no intentions of selling it at any price. You might as well erase it from your little map there."

Jack took a few steps toward the front of the room so his presence would be impossible to miss. He stood quietly as, one by one, other people stood up and offered their comments. Some wanted to know if American would up their offers and if they could negotiate. A few said they had no place else to go. Joe Theobald bluntly told them his ranch was his livelihood and there was no way you can move a ranch somewhere else. It was becoming clear there would not be a unanimous decision to sell off the properties.

When the crowd buzz quieted down Billy Pickett stood up and looked over at me with a grin. I said to Katie, "Uh oh, this oughta be good."

"Mr. Marshall," he began slowly, "Please let me finish my comments. I don't live here so I have no financial stake in what happens. But when I look at the fact American wants to buy up a whole town I just start thinking again about the mining part of all this." He waited a moment for a response from Marshall but when he didn't get one he continued. "Like I told you earlier it's my understanding that the in situ method isn't used for copper. I talked to a couple of friends who have a lot of experience with it. They know like I do that silver and gold are commonly found with copper. My friends have both worked with in situ to mine for silver and one of them has also used it on getting gold out of the ground."

The crowd was listening intently as Billy spoke. It was as if they were reading between the lines. The word gold has a certain power in mining communities. The noise in the room slowly reached a roar. Even Father Riley was shouting at Marshall. It didn't look like Jack was making any moves to quiet things down and Marshall was visibly shaken. When Billy raised his hand the crowd quieted and he continued. "Something else I learned is that in situ recovery can damage an aquifer. That would mean if you begin to inject leaching chemicals in or near a town like Encino you could ruin their water supply."

A desperate Marshall pleaded over the noise of the once again boisterous crowd. "Please, everyone, listen to me. The offers we are making you on page three are very generous. Look at them closely!"

Jack finally got involved. He waved his arms to quiet the crowd and then turned toward Marshall and his group. "Mr. Marshall, I'm gonna level with you. My guess is you people came here tonight thinkin' you'd be talkin' to a bunch of small town rubes. Well, you're wrong. There isn't a person in this room who hasn't already figured out what you're up to. You found more silver, maybe even some gold and you need to use this new kind of minin' to get to it." He paused and looked at each of the nervous looking people in the American group then he turned his back to them and faced the crowd. "Every one of you here tonight is a survivor. American tried to kill our town and we're all that's left. Now they want to buy us out for pennies on the dollar." Every person in the room was nodding. Jack glanced over his shoulder at Marshall then looked back at his friends, neighbors and the other people who had a stake in the outcome. "Folks, to me this kind of feels like we just turned things around. We're all sittin' on a god-damned gold mine. Oh, sorry for the slip, Father. But the way I see it is we have two choices. One, we can stay put, work out the thing with the water, let them hire more workers and keep Encino alive. Or two, make them pay us a whole lot more and leave town with lots of money in our pockets." He paused and looked over at me. "Folks, it's time we draw a line in the sand… or in the dust. It's time for us to make a final stand."

I looked around and saw there were nodding heads and quiet conversations going on around the room. The bankers from Santa Fe were talking to each other. The County Commissioner and Engineer were looking over the offer sheet in the report. Joe Theobald had sat down next to Tom Harmon and the two ranchers were pointing at the map on the projection screen. Saul and Lana walked over and sat down behind Katie and me. "Holy shit, he said, "can you believe all this? Do you think there's really a chance for these people to get their town back?"

I was still trying to get my head around everything that had been said in the last twenty minutes and just answered, "It's a whole new ballgame."

As the surprised crowd continued trying to understand what had just happened I watched as Marshall and his little group started to pack up their laptops and paperwork. They seemed to be in full retreat. Jack stepped toward Marshall and said something but I was out of earshot. All I could figure was that Marshall's head shaking and grim expression were signs that they were leaving and that there might be another meeting or even many of them. Jack extended his hand and Marshall shook it weakly.

Saul and I walked over to the reporter and cameraman. She recognized us from our brief introduction after the silver scandal had gone public. "Wow," she said, "you guys might have another chapter to add to your documentary."

Saul grinned. "Yeah, we'll have to come up with a new title though, something like *Still Not Dead.*"

Keep on Keepin' On

A few of the locals and most of the non-local attendees of the meeting regrouped back at The Bond. It was great watching Russell once again move back and forth between his roles as Innkeeper and Bartender. Father Gerhardt sat at the bar drinking Scotch with the two bankers. The two men from Torrance County shared beer and a table with Billy Pickett. Over in the corner real rancher Joe Theobald sat talking with would-be rancher Tom Harmon, who had donned a Stetson and actually looked authentic. Jack stood quietly at the end of the bar scanning the room with a satisfied smile on his face.

Katie and Lana had gone upstairs to their rooms and when they finally came back down to the bar Lana called out to us, "Hey, it looks like a party!"

Katie chimed in, "Yeah, I thought the same thing. What happened to all those angry people?"

Saul laughed. "I think all that talk about silver and gold put everyone in a good mood."

"This whole evening has been a surprise," I said. "It went from confusion to anger all the way to shock and excitement."

When Saul was finished filling Katie and Lana's wine glasses he offered a toast. "Here's to Encino. May these good people finally get what they deserve."

Katie seemed to be studying my face. "You look, I don't know...happy."

"Oh, I'm just watching Russell and everything that's going on here. It reminds me of those photos my Dad took, back when The Bond was full of people and the town was a different kind of place. That was how Encino came into my life." I enjoyed the hug and kiss on the cheek that Katie gave me. She added, "And you know, if you guys hadn't made the documentary you wouldn't have met Wade and Saul wouldn't have met Lana. It's a freaking love story."

I smiled but tried to manage my expectations. Maybe it was because the story of Encino had taken so many twists and turns that I knew it was too early to celebrate. It felt like things were still up in the air. "Let's not get ahead of ourselves here. A whole lot happened tonight but nothing was really settled. American Mining is still holding all the cards."

"Maybe yes, maybe no," Jack said as he walked over to our table. "Mind if I join you folks?" He grabbed a chair from the next table and sat down. "Thanks again, Jay, for findin' a guy like Billy Pickett. He's the real deal. Whatever American was plannin' to get away with sure came back around to bite em' in the ass."

I grinned. "Yeah, they sure weren't expecting to hear from a guy who knows as much about mining as they do."

Katie added to her earlier comment. "Jack, have you talked to any of the Encino people who were there tonight? They seemed so angry when the meeting started but by the time things wrapped up they were all smiling. What happened? The American Mining people definitely weren't smiling."

"Yeah, after the meetin' I walked out with the crew from KOB and they went straight for the guys from American. She was really drillin' em' with questions and they weren't very talkative. She told me it'll all be on her news show in the mornin'. Jay, you gotta make sure you watch that."

"Oh, don't worry, we'll all be sitting right here watching it before we head back to Albuquerque. Russell says the TV over the bar is already tuned in and the coffee will be ready."

Saul leaned over toward Jack. "I gotta ask, are you all really thinking of selling your properties to American?"

"I guess it depends on who you talk to. The guys from the banks want to get out from under all their empty stores and properties. I can't blame em' for that. But I talked to a couple of people, ones who are still here and hangin' on, and they think they can work out a deal to stay put. And they think there's a bunch of others who want to come back home."

"What kind of a deal?" Katie asked. I was wondering the same thing.

Jack looked around and then lowered his voice. "I can't speak for anyone but myself, but the way I figure it we got American by the balls. Oh, sorry ladies."

Lana smiled and said, "Interesting, keep going."

"Well, after the meetin' I talked to Billy awhile. He says that for them to do that in situ kind of drillin' they need all the land, not just some lots and properties here and there. That's the only way they can control the pumps and get enough of the silver and gold to make it worthwhile. Billy says they wouldn't even be talkin' to us if there wasn't a whole shitload of it down there. Sorry again, ladies."

I had to join in. "So the town and the ranchers are sitting on a silver mine or even a gold mine. They know it and American knows it so now we sit and wait until someone blinks."

Jack nodded. "Yeah, that's pretty much it. It sounds like there's a fortune in the ground under us and everyone wants their own piece of it."

"But what about all of the properties that are vacant?" Saul asked, "There's gold and silver under them too. The banks would try to get in on that part of the deal and the town would still be empty."

"Yeah, I know that. Banks are gonna be banks. But I think everyone who's managed to stick around wants a deal that keeps em' here. Unfortunately that's not enough to give us our town back. We need to find the folks who left, especially the ones who still own their places, and see if they want to come back, and maybe bring some new folks with em'."

"But what would they be coming back to?" I asked.

"Well, for one, they'd be comin' back to a house or a piece of ground that has silver or gold sittin' under it and that means American would have a check waitin' for em'.

"From what we all heard at the meeting the crowd was pissed. They said American and Todd Capital were low balling them. It sounds like it's gonna be a standoff."

Saul downed the rest of his glass and said, "It's like everything's back where it started. Not dead but almost."

A Waiting Game

In its heyday The Bond was considered first class accommodations. Sadly, time and the lack of a reasonable maintenance budget had taken a toll. Russell had kept the place immaculately clean but the mattresses and bedding had aged, the carpet was badly worn and the old wooden floors groaned with every footstep. We all took that in stride and the next morning when we gathered around a barroom table we were in good spirits. Rita had come by to help Russell put together a small buffet. The coffee was waiting and Russell had tuned the television over the bar to KOB in anticipation of the morning newscast.

One by one the handful of others who'd spent the night made their way down to the barroom to join the few locals who'd stopped in to watch the news. Tom Harmon walked over to our table. "Morning, all, is everyone ready to find out what's going on?"

Katie answered, "Well, who knows what we'll find out? That meeting last night ended up being more questions than answers."

"I feel so bad for these people." Lana added, "This is their home. All they want is to have a normal life like everyone else but they're just being jerked around."

When Tom grabbed a chair and sat down with us I said, "You know, Tom, that meeting last night and all of the stuff we found out about was a lot to digest. But I reminded myself this morning that Saul and I are supposed to be here working on your story, the ranch, the stolen artifacts. That's why you came all this way and here we are thinking about nothing but Encino. I apologize."

"Oh, that's okay. I've been thinking about that too and it occurred to me that the two stories just might be connected." He looked around the room and asked, "Don't you think it's strange that guys from American trespassed on my land and drilled their test well just thirty feet from my well, the same well that supposedly was hiding the artifacts?"

Saul nodded. "That occurred to me too, last night when you tried to pin down that Marshall guy about their trespassing. Whoever found the artifacts was trespassing and I have a feeling it wasn't two separate groups."

Katie leaned over to Lana. "Remember our conversation about how every project the guys work on involves bad guys?"

Lana nodded. "Yeah, and just like with Wade's story these bad guys wear suits."

The television had been on but with the sound turned down. We heard Russell call out, "Hey, everyone, it looks like our story's coming on!" He turned up the volume and we all stared at the screen. Linda Ruiz was sitting at the anchor desk with a large photo of downtown Encino on the big screen behind her. We listened as she began her report.

"Our ongoing story of the town of Encino continues to play out. As you know, the small Torrance County mining town that was once home to several thousand people has suffered as American Mining has been slowing down its large open-pit copper operation. Earlier this year we reported that the slowdown was due to a secret silver mining scheme that was exposed during research for a documentary on the town. The scheme was not disclosed to the CEO or Board of Directors and eventually led to the arrest and conviction of a number of American's executives and field workers."

The slide switched to a wide angle view of the mine. "That trial led to public promises from American to recommission the mine, to bring the mining activity back to original levels and to hire more people. It was good news for Encino but it never happened and now we know why."

A video clip appeared, coverage of the meeting at the school. "Last evening a management team from American Mining along with a financial consultant met with a group of Encino residents and property owners. The message the residents were expecting turned out to be very different from the one they got. There was no talk of new hiring or expanding work in the pit. Instead American announced their plan to mine for silver and gold using a new mining method called In-situ Recovery. We asked American's Manager of Southwest Operations, Michael Marshall, about the plan."

A subtle but heartfelt round of boos filled the barroom when the video of a very nervous and uncomfortable looking Marshall appeared on the screen. Saul and I looked at each other and grinned. The KOB broadcast continued. "Mr. Marshall, we reported last year on the silver thefts and the scandal at your Encino copper mine. At that time your company promised to gear up the copper mining activity and to hire back more workers. Has that happened?"

Marshall seemed tongue tied. "Well, yes it has. Uh, actually we're doing things differently now, not like we were doing it before. It's very different now."

It was a non-answer and Linda asked him again, "Has American hired more miners?"

"Uh, well, in a manner of speaking yes. We have brought in experts in what's called In situ Recovery. It's a very exciting new technology/"

"And did those experts come from the Encino area?"

It was obvious that Marshall had no intentions of answering her questions. He began what could only be described as a speech. "This new in situ mining will be a wonderful thing for the people of Encino. The work is done with chemicals underground and it eliminates all of the dust. It's very environmentally friendly." The smug look on his face seemed to say, "There, I answered your goddamn question."

Linda thought otherwise. "There was a man at the meeting who was an experienced miner. He stated that your new method isn't used for copper but could be used for silver and gold. Will you be mining for silver and gold in Encino?"

The color seemed to drain from Marshall's face. Again, he ignored her question. "American Mining and our investment partner, Todd Capital, have made very generous financial offers to the people of Encino to acquire their properties so we can continue operations there."

Linda Ruiz was clearly irritated by Marshall's evasiveness but she persisted. "Another item that came to light at tonight's meeting was that your in situ mining method poses a chemical hazard to the water supply of the town and the surrounding ranches. Can you speak to that?"

Marshall seemed to realize he was overmatched. He struggled to form a polite smile and said, "The people of Encino have our offers and now it's up to them to make their decision. That's really all I have to say at this time." He rudely turned and walked away, off camera.

Linda tried to sum up what had been a very awkward interview. "Well, that was my conversation with Mr. Marshall last evening and as of this morning we have received no further comment from American Mining. There does not appear to be any change to the operating status of the Encino mine. The hopes that the local economy would improve and people would return to their town still seem to be up in the air. We will stay on top of this story and continue our reporting. For KOB News this is Linda Ruiz."

The barroom was silent for a few moments as we all tried to absorb what we'd just seen and heard. Jack stood up and walked over to the bar to refill his coffee. He turned toward us all and said, "I don't know about the rest of you but to me that was nothin' but the same bullshit we've been gettin' from American for a couple of years now."

"Well, not really, Jack." I said, "Maybe it sounded like that but this time around they don't hold all the cards. You folks have something they want and they want it bad. They laid out their little scheme, put an offer on the table and then they stepped back to see how you'd counter it."

A tall, weathered man who I'd seen at the meeting but hadn't met was standing near our table. He took a step toward us and said. "Excuse me for being nosey but I heard what you all are talking about. I'm Pete Pillsbury. I'm Chief Engineer for the County. My interest in this whole thing isn't financial so please understand that. My interest is in making sure that any kind of chemical injections into the soil don't hurt the town water supply or anyone else's aquifers. I checked our files and American never filed for a drilling permit of any kind. That's a very big question mark at this point and there'll be no more drilling of any kind until we do the engineering on it."

"That's good to know," Saul replied. "The guy from American ducked that whole subject."

"Yeah," I added, "I think he figured the subject of buyouts to the property owners would be the only thing anyone cared about."

Pillsbury nodded. "That's the way it seemed to me too, but like you said we're holding all the cards in this game. And I'll repeat, nothing's gonna' happen anywhere until we do a complete engineering review. That's a promise."

His comments made me curious. "So, Pete, how much do you know about water issues like this? Is it possible to measure and isolate an aquifer and then drill around it instead of right into it?"

"Yeah, it can be done. It won't be easy and it would cost a whole lot more but if people, I'm talking about American, will just slow the hell down I think we could make it work."

Jack seemed to like what he'd just heard. "Mr. Pillsbury...Pete, I think we're going to be seein' more of each other these next few months."

Pillsbury offered his hand and replied, "I agree. Now all we have to do is round up everyone who lives here, everyone who wants to move back and then we pull together the banks. Who knows, this town just might come back to life again."

Tom had been sitting quietly, listening to the television and the conversations around him. He looked at Jack and then Pillsbury. "It sounds like this whole things gonna be stuck in neutral until the engineering work is done. That's gonna take awhile, In the meantime I think I have an idea that just might be a game changer."

"Let's hear it" I said.

"Well, from the looks of things that interview put American back on its heels. They look bad and they know it. The stink of their last little crime hasn't even worn off yet. When it comes to public opinion their "save the environment" bullshit isn't a strong enough argument to win out over our "dying little town" story."

Katie leaned in. "So, counselor, it sounds like you've got a strategy."

"It's just an idea but I think it's enough to win the hearts and minds of the people of New Mexico, That is if we can hurry and pull together a media blitz."

I couldn't help but smile. "Ooh, I like the sounds of that."

Jack looked skeptical. "What do you mean by a media blitz? That TV station's doin' about all it can do."

"I mean social media. It's faster and we can target who we want to reach. We have a young marketing intern at my office. She'd be perfect to take this on and I'll pay her to moonlight the whole thing."

Katie was smiling and nodding. "You know, I've been thinking about something you said, Jack. You said it was time to draw a line in the sand and make a final stand. And you're right. And I could see that as the whole theme of the social media thing; *Encino's Last Stand* in big, bold letters and a slogan something like *Drawing a Line in the Dust*. Add a photo of the sad state of the downtown and it's perfect."

Saul added, "Anybody who sees that will be hooked right then and there."

Tom continued. "If we're going to do this right I'm going to need some help, mainly from you, Jack, and the rest of the people here. I'll need whatever contact information you have for all the people living here and whoever else they have kept in touch with. We'll start there and ask those people to spread the word to anyone else tied to Encino."

There was no way to tell how far the Facebook message could reach but it was a good way to get started. Russell brought out a legal pad and a ballpoint pen. It wasn't exactly a high tech way to gather information but within half an hour a surprisingly long list of names had been compiled. Project *Encino's Last Stand* was off and running.

The Best Laid Plans

"Jesus H. Christ, could this thing be any more screwed up? Mike, how in the hell did you lose control of this?"

"Come on, Bill, I had no idea there'd be a damn ringer in that crowd, That guy, Pickett, knew enough about mining to screw up our entire pitch. And Stan, you're the one who put the presentation together, not me. There was nothing in it I could have used to respond to those kinds of questions."

"I saw what Stan put together. It wasn't exactly a work of art but it should have been enough to close the fucking deal."

"Bill, we were ambushed. Those two guys who did that damned Encino documentary were there in the crowd. I think they're the ones behind getting that Pickett guy too. He was the one who knew all about mining gold and silver and he turned the whole crowd against us."

"Mike, you should have just stayed to the script I gave you. The last thing we wanted those people to know was that there's gold and silver under their land. Now we're gonna' have a god-damned gold rush. That land is gonna' wind up costing us a whole lot more than the guys at Todd had figured. If we can even get it."

"Both of you guys had a hand in this mess. I'm already getting calls from people on the Board who saw the news on TV. They want to know what we're going to do to clean it up."

"There's also the water problem to deal with. That reporter tried to pin me down on that and I flat out didn't have an answer. I'm not a god-damned engineer. The plan was to sell in situ as a clean alternative to digging but that damn Pickett guy made it sound like their water was going to be poisoned."

"Look, Mike, and you too Stan. We've got to get back out in front of this while we still can. I'm sick and tired of us being the guys in the black hats. Get our engineers working on the water issue but tell them to stay away from the County guys. Restoring groundwater is a Federal thing and it's tricky and expensive so let's try to avoid having to do that if we can.

"Stan and I were wondering about all the unknown property owners."

"I've got our legal team digging into the status of every little house, shop and vacant lot in that crummy little town. We're going to find out exactly who we'll be fighting with."

"So what do we do next?"

"You find out whose ready to make a deal on their land right now and what it'll take to make a deal with the others. There's a shitload of wealth under that damn town and it looks like we might have to wrestle them for it."

"Okay, I'll get started on it but there's one other thing that could totally screw up our plans. I sat there at that meeting and I watched the expressions on those peoples' faces. I heard everything they said. There were people there who insisted on saving the town and bringing it all back like it was. They're the ones that don't give a shit about the gold or silver. They actually want Encino to go back to the way they remember it. I'm betting they'll fight just as hard as we will."

"You know it wasn't that long ago that a little muscle could have solved this whole problem. You know, put a scare into them. I miss those days."

"No way, forget that kind of shit. This story is out there now, all over the media. We have to do this clean and by the rules. Politically correct in every way."

"Yeah, too bad though, but I still think we have to play hardball, let em' know who's boss."

"Be careful with that kind of talk. It could get out of hand real easily."

"Okay, I guess we'll have to try it your way. Let's get things started."

Encino's Last Stand

Over the next few days I received numerous emails from Tom Harmon. He had gotten his marketing intern working on a Facebook page and even a simple website. Saul and I sent him still photos of the sad state of the town. It included an old newspaper photo of Railroad Street and a current one from the same vantage point. We sent him multiple views of the mine and numerous shots of empty houses and storefronts. With their permission we even included a few photos of some of the local residents.

Pete Pillsbury's engineering effort got underway fairly quickly but he warned us it would be a very long and detailed process. Over the years Torrance County had been somewhat lax in keeping their drawings up to date. Minor changes that didn't mean much at the time were now critical in knowing exactly what was underground. Fortunately the extra time needed to pin down those details would work in favor of Tom's people-search project.

Just when things seemed like they were in a holding pattern an unexpected but welcome bit of news arrived in a voicemail from Jack. He said that all the publicity about the chance of gold and silver under Encino had brought scores of visitors to town. Most were just curious people from nearby towns looking for an afternoon's worth of sightseeing. That wasn't surprising but he said there were other people who showed interest in the empty houses that were on the market. It was only a few people, not enough to call it a Gold Rush, but it was a sign that word was spreading about Encino's predicament.

There was also a steady stream of American Mining executives driving around to all parts of town. They were as tight-lipped as ever. The engineers who came with them were getting in the way of the County engineers so Jack requested that a Sheriff's Deputy stay close by to keep the groups apart.

The best part of Jack's message was that all those people nosing around town were also buying gas at Jack's station, eating meals at Rita's café and even renting rooms at The Bond. It was nice to hear that there was finally something positive happening after two years of bad news. How long that good fortune would last was anyone's guess.

After another week of messages and conversations with Tom we could see real progress from the Facebook page. They had over a thousand likes and nearly a hundred comments. Among those comments were the names and contact information for sixteen former Encino residents. If the town was to survive it would require some of those people to return.

Our conversations also included updates on our research into Tom's ranch and its history. I'd found more information on his great grandfather. Beyond the connection to the ranch's history the information was a treasure trove of facts on the colorful life of an icon of old Hollywood. Tom was grateful for the chance to learn more about his New Mexico roots. He seemed to be settling in to his new role as one of the locals.

For the next three weeks I traded messages and conversations with Jack, Pillsbury and even Billy. The engineering study was moving along more quickly than expected and the Facebook page had become a link to former Encino residents scattered throughout the state. We'd all managed to put together enough information to justify another trip to Encino. Not surprisingly Katie and Lana insisted on joining us. The Encino story had become a compelling and personal effort for everyone who knew about it.

We drove down on a Friday. The crowd of people who'd asked to attend led Jack to once again arrange the meeting at the school. The feeling in the room was the exact opposite of the last time we had all gathered. This time it was just the locals and people with past connections to the town. American Mining wasn't there in the flesh but their shadow still hung over the room. The agenda was an update on the engineering research and clarifications on the ownership of certain downtown properties. The meeting would also include a list of the people who'd resurfaced and had a stake in the outcome.

Jack and Joe Theobald shared the task of running the meeting while Russell took careful notes of everything that was said. Tom Harmon sat in the back of the room with a tape recorder. Saul and I had decided to just sit back and observe the activities. Every single person in the room had something on the line; their home, their property and their future. Their comments were less strident and more hopeful than the first meeting but no one doubted that going up against American Mining would be a battle. There was no doubt that the future of the town could go either way. Encino's Last Stand was taking shape.

What's Next?

On Saturday morning we shared coffee and conversation with Russell and Jack before we hit the road. Our drive back to Albuquerque was an hour and a half of non-stop conversation. Each of us had a slightly different take on what had happened at the meeting but what we all agreed on was that something was finally going to happen. People might move back if the mining generated enough work. If not, the people who stayed and the ones who still owned their properties might see a big windfall from the mineral rights under their feet. That would at least give them time to weigh their options for the future.

I spoke up a little so I'd be heard over the road noise and said, "I talked to Tom Harmon just before we left. He's going to stick around for a day or so and Joe Theobald's going to walk the ranch with him. Tom has volunteered to handle all of the legal stuff that we know is going to happen."

Saul leaned forward from the backseat. "That's good to know. From everything that was said last night this thing feels like it's just getting started. It's probably going to be a battle of lawyers."

"Yeah, and bankers," Katie added. "Now that the story's been on television who knows who will come out of nowhere to stake a claim"

"That's what Jack said to me last night" I said, "He's hoping that some of his old neighbors saw the report and will be hurrying back to their homes. He's got a list of people to contact. The more the original residents can join in the more leverage they'll have against American.

Lana had been quiet since we got on the road and I noticed she was writing something in a large black notebook. "What are you working on back there, Lana?"

She looked up, glanced at Saul and then answered, "Oh, it's just somethin' I do when an idea strikes. I met so many nice people and heard their stories. I saw their town and I felt so bad. Remember when I told you this would make a good Country song? Well, I wrote some lyrics and I have a basic melody for it."

Saul was grinning. "She sang it to me in our room last night and it's beautiful. I told her to reach out to Wade because I think he'd like it enough to record it."

Katie noticed that Lana was blushing and said, "Holy cow, keyboards, songwriting and you can sing too. You've got to let us hear it."

Lana looked at Saul again, sighed and said, "Well, okay, but it's still kind of a rough draft so bear with me."

I slowed down a little and we drove in silence while Lana began:

Empty streets, empty church, and empty houses, once filled with good people and hope. All the things that some said goodbye to, others strugglin' and tryin' to cope.

Nothin' but silence, not a sound anywhere. Just the wind and the dust, always dust. A few hardy souls tryin' to keep things alive, not knowin' who else they can trust.

Encino, how are you doin'? How many were just left behind? Encino, can you keep goin'? What kind of tomorrow will you find?

It's a company town and you know what that means. "It's business" they said, "and that's all." Whatever they gave you they took it all back, and brought the whole town to a crawl.

Encino, how are you doin'? How many were just left behind? Encino, can you keep goin'? What kind of tomorrow will you find?

A handful of you just never gave up. You hung on to the things you were needin'. It's clear your town is the world to you, and the heart of Encino's still beatin'.

Yeah, the heart of Encino's still beatin'.

THE END

Printed in the United States
by Baker & Taylor Publisher Services

Printed in the United States
by Baker & Taylor Publisher Services